A GAME CALLED MURDER

When Dolores Harper went to Puerto Rico to visit her uncle, she met a beachcomber called Whitney Jackson. Together they discovered the grave of a girl who had been murdered a hundred years ago – and shortly after, Dolores's uncle was murdered. After the San Juan police department failed to solve the mysteries, it was up to the beautiful and wealthy widow Rosaria Aldama to pinpoint the relationship between the two killings.

A GAME CALLED MURDER

When Dolores Harper went to Puerto Rico to visit her uncle, she met a beachcomber called Whitney Jackson. Together they discovered the grave of a girl who had been murdered a hundred years ago – and shortly after, Dolores's uncle was murdered. After the San Juan police department failed to solve the mysteries, it was up to the beautiful, and wealthy widow Rosaria Aldama to pinpoint the relationship between the two killings.

A GAME CALLED MURDER

by

Jared Ingersol

Dales Large Print Books
Long Preston, North Yorkshire,
BD23 4ND, England

British Library Cataloguing in Publication Data.

Ingersol, Jared
    A game called murder.

    A catalogue record of this book is
    available from the British Library

    ISBN   1-84262-018-5 pbk

First published in Great Britain by
Robert Hale & Company, 1969

Copyright © 1969 by Robert Hale & Company

Cover photography © J. Allan Cash Photo Library Ltd.

The moral right of the author has been asserted

Published in Large Print 2000 by arrangement with
Robert Hale Ltd.

Dales Large Print is an imprint of Library Magna Books Ltd.

Printed and bound in Great Britain by
T.J. (International) Ltd., Cornwall, PL28 8RW

CONTENTS

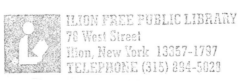

Chapter One

A DIFFERENT WORLD

The Estate Sao Paolo – Saint Paul – was known by the Latin name *castellum* or *castella* for a hundred and fifty years before a holy man living in the decayed ruins gave it a different name, the one it bore when Howard Fitzgerald bought it another hundred and fifty years after the holy man disappeared, some said, lifted directly to heaven by none other than Saint Paul himself.

Because its historic stonework formed a waist-high wall upon the promontory thrusting over the sea, where ceaseless watch was kept for generations against the stealthy approach of sea-pirates, and also because someone, sometime, had mounted three bronze cannon commanding the ocean below and its deep-water channel, Sao Paolo Estate had been known as a *castella*, a fort, which it had never been, nor had there ever been adequate stone construction on the highland cliffs overlooking the approaches to Puerto Rico, to give it even the faintest semblance of such an establishment.

The bronze cannon *had* been fired. Three times at French privateers, twice at American pirates, and innumerable times at those most unpredictable of all, the British buccaneers.

Legends abounded, myths were endless, sagas of courage, of bloodshed, of pillage and rapine chilled the blood of every visitor to the Estate Sao Paolo. Most fortunately Howard Fitzgerald kept what was probably the best-stocked bar in all Puerto Rico. He could thus succour his unnerved guests.

But Puerto Rico and its little neighbouring islands have always been Spanish places, so one was entitled to ask: how did the Estate Sao Paolo get a name which is Portuguese, not Spanish?

The answer, the noble Curate Alfonso Cordoba would say, was ridiculously simple: Because that sainted holy man who had given the place its name had not been Spanish, he had been a Portuguese holy man en route from Lisbon to São Paolo, in Brazil, who had never got where he'd been going, but who'd never given up giving São Paolo as his destination. Father Cordoba, historian, was also a physician.

As far as Howard Fitzgerald was concerned the history of the estate, or for the matter of that the history of Puerto Rico, was unimportant. He was a very wealthy man, and although he might nod with a smile of fixed intensity while listening to some dissertation on the Spanish Main, pirates, hidden gold doubloons or just plain history as it actually happened, he was not likely to be impressed.

In the town of Feliciano which was nearest the Estate Sao Paolo, *el patron* Fitzgerald was accorded the great respect rural people, reared in the old-time Spanish ethos, invariably offered their most wealthy and prominent citizen.

Howard laughed at that, but he did nothing to injure the image, and in fact when Curate Alfonso Cordoba, in the absence of his Father Superior, had the unmitigated brass to suggest a favour, a token for the village from its most honoured nearby *patron,* Howard had asked what would be appropriate.

Little Father Cordoba had said, 'There was a day, *Señor,* when a bell for the church steeple was the desire of each village. Wealthy *patrons,* very often soldiers who had only just taken the money from the people anyway, sent off to Belgium, to Holland, to Britain, for bells whose tones and characters have actually shaped the lives of many, many people.'

'I see,' exclaimed Fitzgerald. 'Then it's to be a bell.'

'Well, *Patron* … no. I only used this as a

means for explaining to you, who are an outsider, how these things came to pass; a little of the history of Puerto Rico, as it were.'

'In that case, Father, would you mind getting to the point?'

'You must forgive me, Mister Fitzgerald. I am a simple man.'

'Yes, indeed. In the same way Machiavelli was simple. Please, Father...?'

'A schoolroom, *Patron*.'

'A *what*?'

'A schoolroom. Feliciano has a very fine bell in the church tower, *Patron*. But the school is very old and very crowded.'

'Quite. And while I also understand *why* Catholic schools are invariably crowded, Father, could you give me some estimate as to the cost of this – schoolroom?'

'As a matter of fact, *Patron*, I just happen to have a cost-estimate in my pocket. The total footage, as you can now see upon this drawing, will be very adequate, even allowing for some increase in the populace.

11

As for the cost – two thousand U.S. dollars. Isn't it ridiculously inexpensive for such a fine addition to the Feliciano school?'

'Well, I suppose church bells cost a fraction as much. Father, it seems I've had the misfortune to be born a hundred years too late.'

'You are very gracious, *Patron.*'

'Is that a fact? It is now taken as a matter of record that I shall endow this building, I take it? Father, the business-world lost an inherently predatory manipulator when you entered the service of the Lord. And one more thing – please stop calling me *patron.*'

'But *Patron,* every village has its *grande señor.* You certainly wouldn't deprive Feliciano... Have you any idea how the other villages would sneer?'

'Father, I have an uneasy feeling that this term *patron* implies more than just respect for some outstanding citizen. Doesn't it also imply that the honoured man is in some measure responsible for a village's needs?'

'Well, of course, in the old days this was

indeed the case.'

'Then please, just refer to me as *Mister Fitzgerald*.'

Little Father Cordoba could agree but that hardly made binding upon the barefoot populace any departure from time-hallowed tradition. Too, endowment of the schoolroom tended to confirm in the public mind that Howard Fitzgerald was indeed Feliciano's *patron*.

The cost of the schoolroom was negligible. Howard Fitzgerald was an extremely wealthy man. When his Last Will and Testament was rendered for probate, those who had not known before were enlightened to the fact that his investments reached all the way from rich mines in Africa to gilt-edged shares in America's largest automobile manufacturing company, not to mention vast tracts of land in California and controlling interest in a securities agency in New York City, with subsidiary offices in Cape Town, Paris and London.

Fitzgerald's attitude towards the school-room endowment had not, actually, been based upon parsimony as much as it had been based upon a disinclination to become involved locally. When he'd acquired Estate Sao Paolo it had been with the idea of enjoying semi-retirement quite apart from the business-world as well as remaining aloof from local affairs.

He told Chester Morrison, his personal secretary, that now he had done his bit of local philanthropy and hereafter he was not available to the local curate, the mayor, the Sisters of Mercy who operated a tin-roofed and mud-floored hospital down in the village, or to anyone else who came up the frangipani-bordered private road leading to the two-thousand-acres of Estate Sao Paolo, seeking alms.

Morrison agreed. He seldom *dis*agreed which doubtless had in some measure been responsible for his tenure; he had been with Howard Fitzgerald eleven years. His word in some spheres was nearly as weighty as the

14

word of his employer since it was well known that he was entitled to speak for Fitzgerald.

Howard Fitzgerald and Chester Morrison were bachelors. That was, as local history indicated, the first time in the lengthy, colourful existence of the Estate Sao Paolo, that such a condition had existed. Always before the Catholic influence had prevailed; alternatively wailing and shrieking women and hordes of children charging through the fields, the groves, even out along the crumbling rampart walls on top of the ageless cliffs.

Also, after four years, the Estate Sao Paolo began to show change. The ancient stone house had its second storey removed, had its lower floor elongated, freshly faced with lovely, quaint local stone, had its mullioned windows re-finished, its serene old patios re-flagged and replanted, its jungle-growth in the flowerbeds and gardens, brought under control.

A swimming-pool had been built and the

little tumbledown chapel with its window of genuine French stained glass, its smooth old stone altar, and four stone pews, had been restored although, except for the cook, the gardener, one or two of the plantation-hands, it was seldom used.

And very gradually Howard Fitzgerald had made something wonderful and exquisite out of the Estate Sao Paolo. It had taken the full four years and a staggering sum of money.

There were several hundred acres in cultivated citrus trees. There also were the row-crops, the herds of pure bred cattle, the experimental plots where skilled agronomists using local peasant labour, struggled to find an answer to a question almost as old as Latin American Man himself – how to feed people who only paused in their eating to ecstatically procreate.

It was Howard Fitzgerald's private world. Although originally he'd been British, at an early age he'd emigrated to the United States, and there he'd been educated – in many ways – and had grown rich. Why he'd never married was anybody's guess. He was a tall man, straight, not quite handsome but presentable enough, and even now in his late fifties, he was vigorous, healthy, alert and urbane.

He had met the world on its terms, had conquered his bit of it, and was now *el patron,* if not by choice of the scruffy little Puerto Rican village of Feliciano, lying at the terminus of his estate, then at least, and by choice, *patron* of the Estate Sao Paolo.

He'd told Morrison that when a man chose to retire, to gently decline, was his own damned business, and *how* he chose to do it was also his own affair. He, a city-dweller all his life, chose this particular way – and corner of the earth – to do both. And of course he'd got so caught up in all the new and exciting undertakings that now he looked better, slept longer and ate less, got so darkly tanned and sinewy, that Morrison's private opinion was that he'd now live to be a hundred.

Howard Fitzgerald was patrician by nature. Not necessarily so by birth, although that too may have been so if he'd cared enough to verify it, but most certainly by nature he was admirably fitted for his new role as lord of the Estate Sao Paolo.

He approved of the small vineyard his people wished to plant near their huts; he even imported a grape-press for them – more sanitary than bare feet tromping out the juice – and he graciously accepted the first dozen bottles of their wine.

He encouraged their little private crafts, allowed himself *in absentia* to become Godfather to their children, and never failed to send gifts to newly-wed couples – provided Hernan' Godoy his overseer told him in time.

Regardless of what he'd said to Morrison or to Alfonso Cordoba about avoiding local involvement, he couldn't have avoided it, because whatever he thought of his personal capacity for making rules, this fresh new world of his was in a part of the world where ancient custom was far stronger than any one man's private desires. Puerto Rico – all Latin America for the matter of that – had absorbed dozens of men like Howard Fitzgerald. It was in the process of absorbing him as well, insidiously and definitely, when he died. And that was a great pity too.

Chapter Two

THE MAN ON THE BEACH

Dolores Harper, Howard Fitzgerald's half-brother's daughter from New England was visiting Puerto Rico for the first time, and being an accomplished horsewoman, was very impressed with her uncle's stable. She volunteered to serve as 'exercise-boy' during her stay, and Fitzgerald was pleased, since he did not have the time – the inclination might have been closer to it – for this chore, although he most certainly recognized the fact that his horses did need an occasional gallop.

Puerto Ricans, qualified to look after horses, were not notable as riders. The historical fates had not made of Puerto Ricans the variety of great horsemen those same fates had made of just about every other Latin American.

There was of course a corollary here; New Englanders had never hacked any deep niches in history from the saddle either. But they at least cultivated riding until it became a flourishing and endemic pastime.

Dolores Harper, like other New Englanders, possessed one facility for riding, she was lean, long-limbed, perfectly co-ordinated and full of confidence; in short, Dolores Harper was poised.

She was also enterprising; the third day of her stay on the estate she completed a ride of the boundary lines. She'd been through jungle, vineyards, groves, pastures, and she'd even ridden out along the forbidding promontory where the crumbling stone walls stood, and where three fat little slumbering bronze cannon, partially hidden beneath the blood-red splendour of wild bougainvillaea, lent their fierce-foolish presence to the legends of the countryside.

She'd also ridden out through the lush

tropical growth below the same shiny cliffs where it was possible to see greeny sea rolling in upon spotless sand, and there she'd followed the fresh-made trail, made by some experienced hand at the rhythmic swing of the machete, and had come upon a cottage in a clearing beyond which, through trees of huge size, one could watch the restless world of trade-winds and sun, sand and sea.

Her uncle, nor his overseer, Hernando Godoy, ever said someone lived down here below the *castella barranca* on the lower limits of the boundary line. Someone did, though. He came silently up behind her horse, carrying his sticky machete, the blade stained with the gummy sap of dozens of varieties of decapitated bushes.

He was fair, although deeply tanned, with wide shoulders, lean hips, a deep chest, and a quiet, composed set of fine features. He was perhaps twenty-five or thirty years of age, but there was something to the depth of his blue eyes that said he had to be much older.

'Don't let me startle you,' he said from fifteen feet back, and in that way positively startled Dolores who had been sitting on her saddle studying the cottage, the thrifty garden, the neat, precise vegetable rows, even the hammock dangling between two trees in all that sea-cooled shade.

He walked on around the horse, keeping a wary eye on it, until he could look up into her face, and she could look down at him as well. He smiled. 'I'm Whitney Jackson; that should be prosaic enough for you. And you'll be Dolores Harper, Mister Fitz-gerald's niece from Massachusetts.'

She was so surprised at the accuracy of this information although she'd only been in Puerto Rico three days, had not been off the Estate Sao Paolo in that time, she blurted out a question.

'How do you know who I am, where I came from?'

He continued to smile and to lean upon that wicked-bladed old machete. 'It's not so difficult. You are a stranger. We get very few in this part of the island. So you see, there is only one of you, but there are a great number of natives. Moreover, you are related to *el patron.* People just naturally take an interest. You should be flattered.'

He straightened up, turned and gestured. 'Please get down, Miss Harper. Have you ever drunk coconut milk? Did you even know such a thing was available anywhere except in the South Seas?'

He was disarmingly pleasant. She dismounted, intrigued, and led the horse along behind her. He had one of those infectious smiles. Also, he was so impersonal it was possible to feel perfectly natural around him. He showed her as they strolled along how the underbrush had been cleared away, or thinned drastically where flowering bushes clung to the tall trees. She said, 'You object to the snakes, Mister Jackson?'

'No. Well, I'm not terribly fond of the snakes, but that's not why I cleared the forest. It's because I like to have perceptive depth when I look at things. This way, I can see a great distance back up through the jungle. It gives a sense of space in all directions around my house.' He laughed, pointed at the cottage and said, 'That's a bold term to use isn't it; I should have said my shack, or perhaps my cabin.'

He had created it himself. He hadn't *built* it, in the literal and technical meaning of that word, because obviously the stone walls with their lichen-stain, had been there hundreds of years, but someone had re-roofed the building, had made a *lanai*, or full-length patio, front and back, and had put in windows, doors, vents, even a chimney and some plumbing. Most certainly the original builder had done none of this; patently, when *that* builder had been around there had been none of these conveniences available in Puerto Rico.

Inside, the cottage was delightful. It was cool and fragrant, artistically furnished and surprisingly clean. She told him he was an excellent housekeeper and he'd said, handing her a coconut-milk punch with a dash of rum in it, that one advantage of living within walking distance of the sea was that by opening both the front and back doors on a windy day, one had no need for dustmops and the like.

He was very easy to be with. He drew her out about her home in New England, about her college-days, even about her vacation at the Estate Sao Paolo. His English was excellent, his humour delightful, his sandalled feet and faded work attire seemed so natural it did not occur to her he might be one of those people who enter the tropics then 'go native', which was to say, live on a level with the peasants, thus earning the scorn both of the natives and their own kind.

And yet, oddly, as she was preparing to ride back home later on, it occurred to her that although he'd drawn her out expertly, he had not in turn volunteered very much about himself. Only his name, actually, and one or two minor things such as how he'd acquired the old stone cottage, how he liked to keep the underbrush pushed back, nothing that lent much insight into his personal life, and whether discretion dictated a ladylike reticence on this subject or not, did not prevent Dolores from being very curious.

She would, she promised herself, find out about Whitney Jackson as soon as she got back to her uncle's mansion; it was improbable that Uncle Howard would know much about a beachcomber, or hippie or whatever Whitney Jackson was, but without much doubt his *major domo,* his overseer, would know. Obviously, this ferreting out of information would prove to be a two-way street.

But prior to her departure, and while the sun was still only part way down its blue-enamel skyscape, he took her out through the cleared forest behind his cottage and part way up the slope to a particular place, and there he showed her what looked like a moderately-sized stone oven, complete with curved roof and great thick walls.

'Crypt,' he said.

She eyed the thing. It had moss and lichen upon it and the stone was glass-smooth from decades of lashing tropical rain. 'Why here?' she asked. 'Or did he perhaps live in your cottage at one time?'

'I think he may have lived there,' explained Jackson. 'I think he was the founder of the Estate Sao Paolo. Look, this old writing; what little can still be made out is Portuguese, not Spanish.'

'How interesting. How did you find it?'

'When I was chopping away at the underbrush. I thought it was a large boulder.'

She turned. The cottage was visible down through the trees, and beyond it, the lonely, restless sea. 'It must have been a favourite place of his. From here he could look out over the sea.' She turned back. 'I know the legend; my uncle wrote my father of it shortly after he bought the estate. Tell me, Mister Whitney; did the holy man yearn most for Portugal or for Brazil? Which direction would he be looking when he'd come here with a heavy heart?'

Whitney Jackson studied her lifted face a moment then inclined his head. 'I think you are here.' He turned to lead her back to where she'd left the horse and for the first time he touched her; he led her along by the hand as though he were leading a child, or perhaps someone he cherished enough to wish some slight warm contact with as they left the ancient crypt.

She asked a question. 'Who put those Portuguese words on his crypt if he was the only Portuguese on the island – and was dead?'

'Oh, the natives I would imagine. He would make the letters for them on a piece of paper, and draw a simple diagram of how and where to put them. The natives would be entirely capable of following those instructions.'

'But, his name...?'

'It isn't there, I'm sorry to say. The only part of the crypt that has rotted away was the bit of plaster over the stone front of the thing where his name was. I've worked a long while sifting the pieces and trying to put them together, but without any real luck.'

He stopped back by the indifferent horse, released her hand and smiled. 'Didn't you wonder what I meant back there when I said I thought you were here, or that you had arrived?'

She toed-in, stepped high, then settled across leather before answering. 'I wondered, yes.'

'I meant ... well, you see, I've lived here a number of years now, and somewhat like our exile the unknown holy man, I know what loneliness is. So I developed this notion that someday a girl would come along. Now does it make sense?'

She nodded. 'Thank you for your hospitality, Mister Jackson.' She reined the horse around and put him back up the trail.

Before she got back to the estate, at least before she reached her uncle's graceful, expensive villa again, the sun was molten red and standing only a few yards above the place where it plunged into the sea each day.

She put up the horse, went to her quarters to change for dinner, then, instead, she slipped into a bathing-suit and ran out to the turquoise pool and dived in.

Her uncle was enjoying a tinkling planter's punch upon the rear verandah and saw her lean figure split the water like the blade of a knife. He smiled nostalgically. Years back he too had been able at the day's end, to dive high and slide beneath the clean water.

When she came out, cool and refreshed – and bedraggled – he called her over, sent one of the silent mahogany servants for another planter's punch highball, and offered her a chaise-longue where dappled sunlight filtered through giant catalpa trees to reach the place where she sat.

'Well, what do you think of *el estado Sao Paolo* by now?' he asked, admiring the fullness, the muscular toughness, of her figure.

'It is heaven,' she said, smiling a little at him. 'Uncle Howard, you have found it – peace, serenity, challenge, opportunity, eternal sunshine. What do you know of a man named Whitney Jackson?'

She ran the two trains of thought together so easily it took him a moment to disassemble them. 'Jackson? Oh yes; Whitney Jackson who lives in the old hermit's cottage just beyond the boundary line, down near the beach. Well, not very much, actually. Some say he's an engineer, some say he's a disillusioned lover, a lawyer, even a doctor. Frankly, as long as his land-clearing projects stops at the property line, Dee, I am not too concerned.'

'But haven't you met him, or spoken to him?'

'I met him once, when Hernan' and I were riding down below the barranca. Didn't have much to say, either of us. He was pleasant, youngish, rather nice looking.'

The servant came with Dolores's highball, smiled and departed. She sipped, found the drink good – but not as pleasant as coconut-milk laced lightly with rum – and sighed.

Her uncle said, 'Have you completed your

survey of the estate?' He was smiling as he asked this, and when she nodded back at him he said, 'Good, because one of these days it will all be yours.'

She looked at him without speaking. She knew of course that her father, a successful New England attorney, was her uncle's only living kinsman, and that she, as her father's only child, was also her uncle's only youthful heir. In a way it was sad; Howard Fitzgerald would have made such a wonderful husband, such an exciting parent.

He said, 'I'm curious, Dee. What will you do with it?'

'Nothing,' she said.

'Nothing? What does that mean?'

'I wouldn't change a thing – and I'd go to the little chapel every now and then so you and I could discuss things – the blight in the oranges, the development of the experimental plots, the condition of the cattle.'

Howard Fitzgerald smiled. 'Good girl. Well, I suppose we'd better go get ready for dinner, hadn't we?'

Chapter Three

AN INSIDIOUS INVOLVEMENT

A man named Frank McFall who was said to own a very large and lucrative car agency in Chicago, had a cliff-hanging villa beyond the village of Feliciano. He was short and burly and robust. He was also bilingual and energetic. He was in every sense of the word a capitalist. He had bought into a boat agency as well as a tourist agency down the coast nearer San Juan, capital of the island. He was seldom still, and in a part of the world where at least some varying degree of languor was inherent, he went his blunt way abrasively stirring things up socially as well as commercially.

He was possibly unacceptable to Howard Fitzgerald, at least socially, although Fitzgerald had undoubtedly known – and used – many men of McFall's character in the business-world, except that in the Feliciano area, if one proposed giving a party, and one selected his guests among the other part-time inhabitants, then Frank McFall became eligible.

And of course there was the priest, Alfonso Cordoba, a very learned and delightful man who could be relied upon to be an ideal guest without permitting his calling or his convictions to boorishly intrude.

And there was also a former territorial governor, John Gore, and Gore's divorced, opinionated son, Frederick, successful in business down at San Juan where he'd been endowed by local wags with the degree Philanderer Cum Laude.

There was also Rosaria Aldama, a wealthy widow of astonishing beauty. At any party Rosaria could be counted among the assets because she was not only beautiful, she was also very keen, very witty, and very capable.

It had been rumoured that she knew more ways to discourage men than any woman in Latin America, which of course may have been taking in a good bit of territory, but on the other hand Rosaria Aldama, being wealthy, had visited every country in the Southern Hemisphere, not to mention all the civilized capitals of Europe as well, and therefore just might have been entitled to her distinction at that.

As Howard Fitzgerald told his niece when he was sending forth the invitations, 'Rosaria is something straight out of the Arabian Nights. If you're expecting one of the dumpy, swarthy matrons of Latin America with their outsized great lumps of shiny black hair, you're in for a surprise.'

Dolores's response had been mildly discouraging. 'But you don't have to hold a reception, Uncle Howard. I could spend my entire month here riding the grounds and–'

'And going native. No, my dear, the heir to Estate Sao Paolo must meet her neighbours.'

'But I'll probably never see a single one of them again. You'll live to be a hundred, I'll marry some balding grocer back in Wooster, and that will be that.'

Fitzgerald had stood looking down at her with a quiet, gentle smile. 'If it would make you feel easier, we could fly in some friends from Massachusetts.'

'Why? Uncle Howard, the tropical sun must have softened you. What kind of New Englander would throw his money around like that?'

'Oh, I suppose an old one might, since there are not very many pockets in a shroud.'

She'd scoffed at him. 'You are not old. Dad told me you were three years younger than he is.'

He laughed at her. 'You have your father's pig-headedness. I'll handle you as I used to handle him. Look, we're going to have the little party and that is final.'

She smiled. *'I'm* pig-headed... All right, we'll have the party. I'll pile my hair on the top of my head, wear a long, white gown and be your regal niece.'

'Splendid. They tell me that one time, more than a hundred years ago, there was a regal lady who ruled the estate. Ask Rosaria Aldama about that legend. She'll know it by heart, more than likely. She's a native and I've been told her people as well as the people of her dead husband have been on the island since the first *conquistadores* landed here.'

'I'll ask. Uncle Howard?'

'Yes?'

'Haven't you overlooked a name on the invitation list?'

Fitzgerald bent to scan the list one more time, brows knit. 'I can't imagine who.'

'Whitney Jackson.'

Fitzgerald raised his face. 'Oh. Well, I suppose it wouldn't do any harm, would it?'

'Why do you say it that way, Uncle Howard?'

'I – uh – have heard that he runs round in sandals and that he actually is some kind of beachcomber. Not that I object, mind, but on the other hand these people are quite different. No sense in embarrassing either Mister Jackson or the others, is there, if it can be avoided.'

She said, 'I'll ride down this afternoon and tell him he's invited.'

'Well...'

'And no sandals, no hippie beads, no beard,' she smiled and patted her uncle's shoulder. 'No holding forth on the spirituality of transcendental meditation. All right?'

'All right, Dee. By the way, what *is* transcendental meditation?'

It was an opportunity to saddle one of the horses which only she and the stableman, Gregorio, cherished. Old Gregorio was a Cuban; his feeling for horses was great but until the arrival of *el patron's* niece he'd been a taciturn, neglected husbandman upon the estate. Now though, he gabbled like a wrinkled old turkey-buzzard, which he to some degree resembled, and laughed often.

He and Dolores got along famously. He was a man of sixty although he did not know, exactly, what his age was, and although unmarried and childless, made the clucking sounds of a grandfather when Dolores would take one of the most nettlesome horses and disappear upon it through the groves and into the jungle growth. He was always a little worried about her.

He needn't have been. By the time the most fractious of the horses got as far along as the old *castella* promonotory where the trail dipped downward towards the sand and the rolling surf, she'd have everything under control. And as she'd told old Gregorio more than once, there was no way for a runaway-horse to get the bit in his teeth and race away headlong, because invariably there was that solid wall of tangled green.

Only down where Whitney Jackson had brushed the undergrowth away, was there that much open country, and even there the trees or, ultimately, the surf itself, would stop a free-racing horse.

When she made the last twist in the downward trail, this trip, the nettlesome mount was sweating and tiring. She was in no hurry. It was slightly less than mid-afternoon.

Evidently Jackson had heard her coming, as he'd done that other time, because he came along the sidehill from the direction of the crypt, shovel over one shoulder, grimy and sweaty from hard labour, but smiling that gentle, serene smile.

She looked concerned. 'You haven't been *digging* up there?'

He leaned upon his shovel, shook his head and laughed at her. 'In the crypt? Good Lord, no. What kind of person do you think I am? There is a spring up the slope a ways. I'm not even sure it's not on your uncle's land, but I got hold of some plastic pipe – as precious as gold – and I'm trenching it by hand down to the cottage. It will be my running water. Think of it – a shower every night.'

She smiled back. 'From the looks of you now I think it might be an excellent idea. What I rode over for – my uncle is giving a party and you are most cordially invited.'

His smile wavered, then faded away. He leaned there, tall, lean, physically fit, studying her. 'I don't know your uncle. I met him once, when he was out riding.'

'What of it? We want you to come.'

'I couldn't.'

'Why not?'

'Well, how would I get there, for example? There is only the trail and can't you just imagine me hiking two or three miles along *that*, in a suit, shoes and tie.'

'A very poor excuse, Mister Jackson. From here to the promontory is no more than a half mile.'

'You're not holding a party there, surely.'

'No. But there is a road to the old fort, and I'll pick you up there in one of the Land Rovers. I'll also bring you back afterwards.'

He said, 'You are my lady of the forest. Can't we just keep it like that?'

She didn't like having to force him to comply so she said, a trifle coolly, 'If you wish, of course,' and shortened the hold on her reins.

'Well look,' he said, speaking swiftly. 'Of course I'll come if you want it, but I'll be very out of place with the others.'

'How do you know that; do you know who'll be there besides you, my uncle and me?'

'No. And I'm sorry if I've disappointed you, made you angry.'

She relented a little. He wasn't a person to be angry with. 'You won't be out of place and I promise not to neglect you. Mister Jackson, it just isn't good for a man to be a hermit.'

His smile returned. 'I had no idea you were a psychologist.' He was teasing her, obviously, but he had a way of doing it without angering her. 'And doubtless what you say is right. But if I were a native I'd find you to be quite contradictory. You see, the name Dolores is Spanish and it means someone who is sad, melancholy, grieving. We have the same thing in English, only it's not a name and it's spelt differently. D-o-l-o-r-o-u-s. You are always full of vitality, quick to smile. Do you see the contradiction?'

'I see it. What does it have to do with you coming to the party?'

He laughed aloud. 'Nothing. And you're certainly a genuine New Englander. Never deviate, permit no digression; hew to the line, always.' He shouldered the shovel and pointed on down the path. 'I've something to show you, come along.'

She hesitated then shook her head. 'I'll have to start back or it'll be dark when I get home. Could you show me some other time?'

'Of course,' he smiled. 'By the way, when is this party?'

She told him, reiterated her willingness to come and get him, then departed back up the shadowy trail with the sun beginning to redden and drop down its great blank place.

Not until she was within sight of the villa did she recall something: she'd neglected to mention attire. She tried reassuring herself that no one who was so obviously a gentleman, would arrive looking *too* odd, but it was no good because she'd read enormously well-reasoned books by men whose pictures on the back-flap showed terrible non-conformity.

By the time she got to the dining-room for dinner she was genuinely worried. Even though he *did* meet her in conservative dress, living down there as he did with no means of going to any of the larger towns, it was fair to assume that his clothing would not be of too recent vintage.

When her uncle asked about the worried expression she told him. He didn't laugh. He ate and after a bit he said, 'We can handle it. I'm going to San Juan tomorrow on business anyway. I'll pick up some things you can take down to him.' Then the calm, wise grey eyes lifted to her face. 'Is this a consequence of inviting him, or do you want him to impress the others as a consequence of liking him?'

She coloured a little. 'What do you mean?'

'You ride down there quite often. He's young enough, and the Lord knows that's one thing there's a shortage of on the estate – compatible young people … young *men*. Dee, it's perfectly all right with me. I am just curious that's all.'

'It's a consequence of inviting him,' she said rather firmly. 'I thought, on the way home, that perhaps that's why he didn't want to attend – because he wouldn't have the proper things to wear.'

'No cause for worry, then,' said her uncle, and changed the subject, although it was fair to assume that neither of them, in fact, *forgot* the subject.

Later, alone on the moonlit front patio with the drowsy call of Puerto Rico's large green parrots to break the languid silence of a fragrant, heavy night, she had a fresh worry: how to hand Whitney Jackson the packages her uncle would bring back from the capital without having him turn brick red and explode at what most certainly would look like largesse from the landed aristocracy to a peasant.

In the end, she wondered why she'd ever got involved in the first place, but that didn't help much; she *was involved,* and that was what mattered.

Chapter Four

ROSARIA

Rosaria Aldama was everything her uncle had hinted at, or had specifically said she was. Dolores was reading a letter from Massachusetts when the low-slung sports car, cream-coloured and shiny, curved into the arching drive and eventually halted out in the front. Dolores guessed who her guest was before Rosaria had alighted – in jodhpurs of soft beige and a blouse to match – and smiled up at Dolores.

Rosaria was a sophisticated thirty-five or thirty-eight but with a golden skin so flawless Dolores found it difficult to imagine her being over thirty. She was tallish, too, and high-breasted. When she moved there was an instantly noticeable sinuous grace as though Rosaria's long legs were very strong.

She introduced herself, said Dolores's uncle had stopped at her hacienda on the way to San Juan, suggesting that Rosaria go on up and visit his niece. Rosaria made it sound almost mischievous, instead of patronizing. Her dark eyes, rather golden than brown, were lively and perfectly unaffected. She was one of those very rare beautiful and wealthy women – perfectly natural.

Dolores liked her the moment they sat down side by side in the shade of the patio. She felt at ease, as though they were old friends, and that, too, was another of Rosaria Aldama's capabilities; she made everyone feel that way, including men, so it was very probable that she had indeed received more than her share of ardent proposals of marriage, as it was said was the case.

She studied Dolores smiling, then said, 'It all is agreeing very well with you.

Sometimes the heat, the humidity, the entire environment, is too different for New Englanders. Of course your uncle has made the transition very well, but then men are different. I'm glad you like Puerto Rica, Dolores; if you hadn't liked it we would be sitting here a bit stiffly, I'm afraid.'

'I love it,' Dolores confessed. 'All of it. It's paradise.'

Rosaria's beautiful eyes softened. 'It will love you, too. You see, with your name it was only right that you should come here.'

Dolores recalled something. 'I'm afraid the name is a contradiction. I was told that yesterday.'

'Not really, one doesn't have to go around with a big, long face because of the name. That's left over from the days when the church ruled with an iron hand and girls weren't allowed to forget the Crown of Thorns. Who told you it was a contradiction?' The golden eyes were fixed on Dolores's face now, steady, wise, perhaps even knowing.

'A man who lives down near the beach below the old walled-up fort. Whitney Jackson.'

'Yes, of course,' murmured Rosaria, showing neither unfamiliarity with the name, or surprise at having it mentioned now.

Dolores, catching a hint of the mood, said, 'Do you know him?'

'I suppose everyone knows Whitney Jackson to some degree,' answered the beautiful woman. 'He has been here five or six years now, and in a place no larger than Feliciano, or a countryside as static as ours, we get to know people as well as we choose.'

Dolores could hardly mistake the cool tone. Ordinarily she probably would have changed the subject. Now she said, 'Tell me about him.'

The golden eyes came to rest upon a distant place beyond the patio, the flawless face was calm, and yet there was something – a harshness – in the underlying expression.

'There isn't very much, I'm afraid. At any rate it is mostly peasant gossip. And as I said, one gets to know as much as one chooses. He came here in a motor launch from Cuba.'

Dolores was startled. She had never for a moment thought of him as anything but an American. Perhaps a middle-westerner. 'Cuba?' she said. 'How odd.'

'Odd? Why odd?' asked Rosaria Aldama. 'Oh, I see, because he is not a Cuban. Well, you and I can *see* that much, can't we, but then being a Cuban for the past ten years or so is less a matter of ethnic grouping than it has been a state of mind. Perhaps Whitney Jackson is a communist at heart. That's what a Cuban is now. In any case, he arrived here in his boat one day, and the very next day, so I have been told, the boat disappeared. He has been here ever since, practically in the same spot, as a matter of fact.'

'Sounds terribly mysterious,' said Dolores. Rosaria smiled. 'It is. But what is even more mysterious, he had several boxes of women's clothing with him when he arrived. Even the jewellery.' The golden eyes lingered on Dolores. 'The peasants say he flung her out of his boat and drowned her on his way from Cuba.'

'Do you believe that?'

Rosaria shrugged. 'I don't particularly believe *any* of it, and yet for five years now none of it has changed. That's about the only way you can be sure there is any truth at all in peasant-talk.'

Dolores rallied, called a servant and had cold drinks brought. She let go of the subject of Whitney Jackson for a while, and asked questions about other things. In this manner she made a startling discovery: the original developers and owners of the Estate Sao Paolo after the disappearance of the holy man had been the Aldama family, the ancestors of Rosaria's dead husband.

Rosaria told her several legends. One had to do with the reappearance of her dead husband's great-grandmother at all the receptions, all the parties given in the main house. The other had to do with a persistent whispering among the older peasants that the holy man hadn't actually been taken off by a saint at all; that he left instructions how and where he was to be buried, along with several oaken lockers which had come to the island with him, and that he had even built his own tomb somewhere on the back side of the island.

Dolores almost told Rosaria Aldama that Whitney Jackson, in hacking away the jungle, had as a matter of fact come upon a crypt. She would have told her except that the servant came with cold drinks and fruit, and afterwards Rosaria was telling an amusing anecdote concerning another of the Aldamas, this time her defunct husband's grandfather, who had been born in the very house at their back over a hundred years before.

'His wife locked him in a stone granary which used to be out back every time a particular band of roving players came to

Feliciano. He was wildly infatuated with one of them – a gypsy, they say, although I'd suspect she was just an Indian because we've never had gypsies in Puerto Rico. His wife would command two of the largest peasants to sneak up and seize him, then carry him kicking and screaming to the stone granary.'

Dolores was amused. She and Rosaria laughed, then it was time for the older woman to depart, so Dolores strolled down to the handsome sports car with her.

Nothing more was said of Whitney Jackson. Rosaria promised to return the afternoon of the party and lend a hand. As she was driving away Dolores caught her little warm wave, and waved back. Rosaria Aldama had made a very favourable impression. She always would, no matter where she went. She was simply that kind of a person.

Later, Dolores went down to the stable where she found Gregorio snoring in a huge hammock of laced cord which resembled one of those big nets people used to drop upon wild animals. He had once explained to her that this was a Yucatan hammock, or bed, for everyone slept in one of them, and also, aside from being completely ventilated, being woven cord, it was also large enough so that no one could fall and be hurt in his sleep. Then too, he'd pointed with pride to the utilitarian aspect of his Mexican hammock.

'*Señorita,* it is only necessary to wash the thing perhaps once or twice in a man's lifetime. Now isn't that a splendid bit of genius, a bed that requires no care?'

She looked at him lying there now, for all the world like a crumpled fly caught in the web of a spider, and smiled. Back in New England poor Gregorio would suffer chills even in July and August. He was truly a child of the sun.

She saddled a horse, led it forth with considerable care so as not to make noise, then mounted it and rode slowly over towards the citrus groves.

The men whistled over there, and laughed, their sparkling Spanish lifting and falling, their endless jokes at one another's expense, brightening every toiling hour.

But they were indeed men; it was always best for a woman to let men know she was in the area. Dolores understood Spanish fairly well, so as she loped easily into sight she distinctly heard the sly allusion made to some woman which brought musical laughter in among the trees. Then, the little trilling whistle of warning, and dark faces popped around trees here and there.

The men were gallant; they waved and she waved back.

There was a certain tameness to the citrus groves. The smell was different, the ground cultivated, the trees grew in perfect rows, everything was orderly. The jungle, which loomed darkly green and distant, was altogether different. Even the eternal Puerto Rican parrot, a big, vivid-coloured bird who always had some view to express, although he visited the citrus groves, doing some malicious damage, preferred the darker, more matted jungle where the scent was of decaying vegetation, not orange blossoms.

Dolores admired the groves as she also admired the planted pastures, but the jungle-fringe was her real delight. There was nothing like it in Massachusetts. Not even in the books one encountered in Massachusetts. It was the primeval world to Dolores; the land before Man, the steamy eons before time. It was full of strange life and although she'd been told there were no snakes in Puerto Rico, she had seen several.

Not this particular day, however, because she did not penetrate very deeply into the jungle. There were only a few trails, cut by the natives on their own time, usually to go from compound to compound, or perhaps to take a circuitous route to the village without being seen.

She had rather well explored all the jungle to the north and east of the estate anyway. Moreover, the jungle on the promontory-side of the cultivated land was thicker, wilder, more remote and less susceptible to change. She thought it must be about as it always had been. Obviously some of the trees were massive enough to be hundreds of years old.

After riding in the opposite direction for an hour or so, she turned like a magnet drawn to a lodestone, and went down towards the promontory. There, she took the trail leading downward, but instead of going as far down as the cleared land, she left the horse tied and went off by herself, into the jungle. She did not wish to be seen. It had nothing to do with what she was about; she simply didn't want to have to face Whitney Jackson again so soon.

The crypt was there. She came down to it from the higher side of the slope. She stood looking at the thing. It seemed odd that the natives, who seemed to have eyes for everything else that happened on the island, had not as yet discovered that Whitney Jackson had found this ugly funerary stone-pile, had cleared the brush away from it.

But perhaps there was an explanation. In the first place, the crypt was off any beaten trail. Rather far off, in fact. In the second place, there would be no reason for anyone to come up here.

She went closer, studied the faint letters, ran a hand over the rough lichen, coarser by far to the touch than any of the cool, ancient stones, and stopped before the perfect fit of the sculptured piece of granite that plugged the final hole in the crypt. It was ingeniously embedded.

After what Rosaria Aldama had said, it was more than just likely that whatever was interred with the holy man's bones would answer all the questions Whitney Jackson was interested in having answered.

On the other hand, this mystery kept him absorbed. What would take its place if he knew all the answers?

She went slowly back to the patient horse trying to arrive at a decision to tell him or not to tell him. She never made the decision. She thought she had to first know other things about Whitney Jackson. After all, except for a slightly cool appraisal by her uncle and a none-too-flattering intimation by exquisite Rosaria Aldama, she knew nothing.

The sun was near to setting when she put up the horse. Gregorio was no longer in his huge, baggy old hammock. He was, she thought, probably somewhere near the kitchen of the main house cajoling some laughing woman into feeding him.

Dolores went to her quarters, bathed, dressed very leisurely, and by the time she was finished the sound of her uncle's car was audible. She hastened out to meet him.

Chapter Five

A MEETING ON THE PROMONTORY

The clothes her uncle had brought back were not only of excellent quality, they were also of modern cut and style. As he showed them to her he said he was fairly certain the size must be about right, but if alterations were required there was a seamstress, a *Señora* Cortez, in Feliciano who could do the job expertly enough.

He then left the things lying on the sofa and turned to ask if Rosaria Aldama had called. Dolores said she had indeed called, that they'd had a very nice visit, and that she was very taken with Rosaria. Her uncle smiled, a trifle absently it seemed, and said he wasn't the least surprised. That everyone liked Rosaria. He then went to bathe and change for dinner, leaving Dolores pondering the masculine clothes draped over the sofa.

She had no difficulty at all imagining Whitney Jackson in those things; he would look handsome, but the obstacle of getting him to accept them loomed larger now than it ever had.

Later, at supper, her uncle showed that he'd also given this matter some thought. 'You have two options,' he said. 'Either hand them to him and immediately ride away – in which case he may throw them down. Or act very innocent, as though you had no idea a man could be indignant over a gift from a girl.' Fitzgerald's grey, wise eyes were sardonic as he said this. 'I don't imagine he's that gullible, and I'll have to tell you honestly that you just don't look that naïve, but there they are, Dee. Unless of course in my absence you've come up with something more wily. After all, you *are* a woman, and if there is one thing I've learned about women over the years, it is that they can be very clever at times.'

He smiled and resumed his meal, his attitude seeming to indicate that he had done his part, from here on it was up to her. Moments later he said, 'By the way, I ran into Fred Gore in the city and extended a verbal invitation. He's the former governor's son, you'll recall.' Again the clear, piercing eyes were sardonic. 'He accepted in a flash, and in the course of the ensuing talk he said he'd heard glowing things about the beauty of my niece … Fred, aside from having been married a time or two, is reputed to be a genuine island lady-killer.'

Dolores smiled. 'You have them here too?'

Fitzgerald smiled. 'Glad to know you can handle 'em. Frankly, I worried a bit on the drive back.'

They went out on to the front patio after dinner, which her uncle looked forward to doing every evening; from this vantage point he could look out over the groves, the pastures, and see also the little thin tendrils of smoke coming from the help-cottages that were hidden beyond the groves. It was a very peaceful, pastoral scene. Except for the parrots it would also have been a quiet one.

Tonight, someone in the distance was playing a guitar. The song, whatever its name, assuming that it *had* a name although in Puerto Rico that was not necessary, had the peculiar sound of transplanted Spanish gloominess. There was an occasional lilt as of golden laughter also, purely native Puerto Rican, so the music was native; it was also, as was largely true of all Latin American music, a kind of hybrid symbolism for the two halves of the whole that signified the background of Castile as well as the good humour of the native.

Dolores listened carefully. Her uncle, seeing this, said, 'I suppose it's normal for people to view with suspicion anything that is different, but most of all, *people* who are different. After living here so long I have a theory: listen to the music of a land and you'll find that people aren't very different, only their emotions are arranged differently. You and I, for example, come of stock that does not readily show much emotion. But we *feel* it. These people on the other hand, *show* it very openly, and so we say they are emotional, while they say we are cold. Actually, we aren't different except in the way our feelings are arranged.'

He laughed.

'You see – I've lived here so long I've become a rustic philosopher.' He turned the subject. 'Well, how will you present Mister Jackson with his new clothes?'

'I wish I knew, Uncle Howard.'

'Suppose I go and do it for you.'

That, she was sure, would make matters worse. 'No thanks. It's my headache. But he'll know you picked the clothes.'

'Will he? Do you know him that well?'

She let the questions go by without answering them. 'Did you hear that he'd come here from Cuba? That he – didn't come alone?'

Her uncle frowned in heavy concentration. 'I don't really recall, Dee. I've been awfully busy here the last few years. And except for that accidental encounter one time, I've never had much occasion to pay attention. Hernan' might know more. You could ask him.' Her uncle turned. 'From Cuba? Is that what the natives say?'

'That's what Rosaria told me today. That he supposedly came here in a motor launch.' She didn't mention again that he may not have come alone, the intimation behind that suggestion being too lurid.

Fitzgerald turned this over in his mind but apparently found it only mildly displeasing because he said, 'Well, he certainly isn't a Cuban, although there are plenty of them in Puerto Rico now, the Lord knows.'

The music stopped, a dog barked beyond the groves, two garrulous parrots made ugly sounds at one another, their voices being a great contrast to their elegant plumage, and her uncle said the local parrots actually did not make very good pets.

'Too stupid, or if they aren't that, then they're too disagreeable. And they bite like the devil too. Every few days some child comes in with a mangled finger or a torn cheek.'

The talk was easy, comfortable, the way it should be after a good meal, but Dolores could feel the hours slipping past towards the time when she'd have to hand Whitney Jackson the packages. Later, after both she and her uncle had retired, she sat by a window in the warm starlight and wondered once again why she'd ever got involved.

The answer remained unchanged. *She had,* and that was that!

The following morning, after her uncle had gone off in one of the Land Rovers with his *mayor domo,* the quiet, smiling, dark and husky Hernando Godoy, she took the packages to the stable, resolutely saddled a horse, and with a wave to old Gregorio, rode off in the direction of the promontory.

She was in no hurry, the morning was fragrant, golden, cool, with sea-breezes coming up over the granite headlands. But after all, the distance was not very great, either, so eventually she came to the place where the trail veered off, either heading down to the beach or out upon the promontory. Movement made her stop. She had detected it from the corner of her eye about the same moment her horse had also detected it.

Whitney Jackson was looking at her from over near a flaming-red, flourishing bougainvillaea vine. He waved and she reined over towards him. As though explaining his presence up there, he gestured towards the three fat, smooth little brass cannons and smiled.

'Privateer off the beach. Probably La Fitte from Louisiana.'

She laughed, dismounted and went over to gaze at the little guns. They had been dowelled into place by someone who had never meant them to be removed. Otherwise, undoubtedly by now some souvenir-hunter or scrap-iron dealer would certainly have carried them off.

The sea was a pale green in close, indicating shoals for a mile or so off-shore, but afterwards it was a steely, shiny blue that became darker the farther out one looked. It was still today, scarcely responding to the under-water currents, and white birds hovered just above it, seeking minnows near the surface. Altogether, the promontory was a beautiful spot, clear of undergrowth, sparkling in the sun, cooled by the sea.

She turned as he dug something from a pocket and offered it. 'I told you I had something to show you,' he said.

She had forgotten, but now, taking the small object from him, she remembered. She also remembered something else – those packages tied to her saddle.

The object he'd handed her was a stone, pear-shaped with a flattened head upon which were several deeply carved lines and letters. It looked quite old. She had no idea what it might be and asked.

He said, 'It's a map, I should judge. I was

waiting for you to go with me to find out what it means.'

'Where did you find it?'

'In the crotch of a tree over near the crypt while I was brushing-out. It had been set there as a sailor might set his binnacle – his compass-box – with that longest line pointing towards my cottage.'

She looked up. 'Buried treasure – in this day and age?'

'I have no idea, but while I've been waiting for you to return I ran off some measurements on a piece of paper. In fact, I've worked out the legend, and if you've the time we can go to the exact spot the map leads to. I drove a stake where it is – whatever it is.'

She handed back the stone. She had plenty of time. She also had a misgiving. 'Maybe it's another grave.'

'In that case we won't bother it, will we?'

She saw her horse move, saw the packages, and taking firm hold of her resolve, said, 'Would you do something for me?'

His reply was instantaneous. 'Of course. What?'

'Those bundles on the saddle.' She felt the warm metal of the nearest little cannon. It was as smooth as glass. 'They are some things for you.'

He looked from the horse back to her, moving his head slowly and still holding the stone. He said, 'I see.'

She risked a look. He didn't *look* angry but it was difficult to tell with him. In a small voice she said, 'Will you be mad?'

'Clothing?'

'Yes.'

He sighed, considered the stone a moment, then dropped it into a pocket and turned to study the burdened saddle again. Finally he said, 'All right. No, I won't be mad. But I'll pay you. Otherwise, you see, I *will* be mad.'

She nodded, feeling enormous relief. She also smiled. 'My uncle made the selections, as you'll guess. I only died a hundred times riding down here to get you to take them.'

He seemed to understand that because he looked at her with a little wry twist to his usual smile, as though except for the way he knew she'd felt, he'd have had some pointed things to say.

She got away from additional discussion of the bundles by saying, 'If you've already figured out what the stone-map means, why didn't you just go ahead and dig up whatever is there?'

'I told you,' he answered. 'I was waiting for you to return.'

She said, 'Oh. Well, suppose we go down there right now.' She thought of what Rosaria Aldama had told her of the holy man's grave and said, 'By the way, did you know some wooden casks or something, according to old island legend, are supposedly inside the crypt with the priest – or whatever he was?'

He nodded. 'I've heard that.'

'You weren't curious?'

'Yes. But grave-robbing doesn't have much appeal to me.'

She was surprised. 'You mean you're not going to open the crypt?'

'Would you?'

'Of course I would. I wouldn't disturb the bones, but whatever else is in there can't do anyone any good buried, can it?'

'No.' He thought a moment then said, 'All right. I'll open the thing if you'll help.'

She looked at him with a forming frown. 'What kind of help? I don't have to look in there, do I?'

He laughed, took her by the arm and started her moving. They got the horse and led him along as they left the promontory and started down the little pathway to the cleared land below.

She was emboldened by her success with the clothing so she asked a question that was in the forefront of her mind. 'Tell me something: why is a man as obviously educated, intelligent, talented as you are, hiding yourself down in this place?'

He kept right on walking, still holding her arm. 'If you really want to know after we dig up our treasure – or whatever – and after we look into the crypt, I'll tell you.'

'Why then?'

'Well,' he said, 'by then you'll be hardened to shocks.'

She threw him a sidelong glance, not especially liking the sound of that.

Chapter Six

AN OPEN GRAVE

According to his measurements the stone-map had indicated a place less than a hundred feet from his cottage, and back up the rearward slope a few yards. He suggested that whatever had been put down there, had been deposited in a position where rising tides could not reach it. He said, 'A sailor would think of that.'

She considered the stake driven in the ground. 'Blackbeard. He's the only treasure-burying gentleman I know.'

He smiled, plucked the shovel off a tree where it'd been leaning and made a stab at the earth. 'You must have heard of buried treasure along the New England coast,' he said.

She didn't dispute that, only her connection with it. 'My father is an attorney, not a seaman, and we live in a town that is quite a distance from the sea. I recall hearing a tale or two as a child, but,' she made a gesture towards the deepening pit at his feet, 'I've never even known anyone who dug for anything like this before. I'm not too sure I'd ever admit to having done so myself. People would think I was insane.'

'Sooner or later they think that of everyone, anyway,' he said, shifting position as he dug, keeping his face from her. 'Never be too concerned about what people think.'

This statement brought back her personal interest in him. It was no longer a simple curiosity but she had no occasion to speculate on the difference between a woman who was curious about a man, and one who is interested in him.

He said, 'I think we've hit it, and by George I think you're right. It looks like a grave. Not a very deep nor elegant one though.'

She didn't get much closer. He began expanding the hole he'd dug. It was about two and a half feet deep which was indeed rather shallow for a grave. He said it may have been dug in a hurry, or under some circumstances that prevented the digger from wanting to go any deeper.

He finally had the full length of the thing outlined enough for her to distinguish the shape. It was just about right for a human body and although there was no coffin, at least not in the conventional sense, whatever lay there had been wrapped mummy-like in what seemed to be an old boat-sail or some such bit of coarse cloth, while beneath that was another wrapping.

But Whitney made no immediate move to press his investigation. He stepped up out of the hole and stood with Dolores, looking down. She asked if he thought it was a human body. He said he was quite sure it was. She asked if he meant to unwrap it and he looked at her.

'Would you?'

'Certainly not!'

'Then I'll just cover it and we can forget about it.'

'Wait, Whitney. You asked if *I* would unwrap it. I meant I would not *unwrap* it. But that doesn't mean you can't, does it?'

He looked down at her. She was defensive at once. Pointing to the position of the body, the evident haste involved in burying it, she said, 'Isn't it a rather unusual burial, even for Puerto Rico?'

He didn't answer but he stepped down into the hole again, pulled his gloves on and went to work with a knife, slicing through the wrappings. What he ultimately found was a mummified, calcified arm with a golden bracelet on it, a shrivelled bosom with an exquisite old brooch holding together several folds of old lace, and a locket round the discoloured, stringy neck that had a tiny oil portrait inside of a girl with huge dark eyes, hair that formed a widow's peak in jet black, and skin the colour of fresh cream. None of the jewellery had been injured through its long burial, thanks of course to all the wrappings.

When Whitney handed out the last salvageable item, the locket, he reached for his shovel to fill the hole in. Dolores, intently examining their finds, was too occupied to heed his labours and when they were finished she had no answers at all, only more questions. He led the way on down to the cottage, tied the horse outside, took the packages inside and tossed them in a chair, then went to wash.

When he returned she said, 'Who were the Montoyas?'

He held out his hand for the locket she was holding. The name was engraved on the left-hand leaf of the locket, opposite the delicate portrait. Angelina Montoya. He shook his head.

'I have no idea. But that was Angelina in the grave.' He handed back the locket, examined the bracelet and brooch, and also returned them to her. They were simply very handsome, and probably very valuable, bits of jewellery, but they were not personalized.

'Heirlooms,' he murmured. 'Would you care for a drink of something cold?'

She declined so he sat down and considered his strong, calloused hands. She caught his mood and said, 'What are you thinking, Whitney?'

Without looking up he answered quietly. 'She was murdered, Dolores.' Into the silence that ensued he rubbed both palms together. 'There was a pretty bad hole in the side of her head as though perhaps someone had come up behind her and fired as she was turning.' He raised up and leaned back in the chair. 'Looks like we've stumbled on to an island mystery.'

'Wasn't the dress – very elegant?'

'Yes. White lace, long and I'd say probably quite expensive. Old, perhaps a hundred or more years old.'

She said, 'What should we do?'

'Nothing. And I don't think it would be too wise to tell anyone about this.' He gazed steadily across the pleasant room. 'Why did someone go to all the trouble of putting the marker in the tree? Murderers usually want to *conceal* a crime, don't they? Someone, someday, had to stumble on to that stone, trace out the directions and dig.'

Dolores put the jewellery aside. She'd forgotten the bundles until she now turned and caught sight of them where he'd placed them. Without sounding very enthusiastic she said, 'Hadn't you better try on the clothes?'

He roused himself, considered the packages and nodded, also without enthusiasm. 'Yes, I suppose so. The party is tomorrow evening?'

'Yes. Whitney? Was she young?'

'Young and beautiful. It's depressing. I wish I hadn't found the damned stone.'

She nodded quiet agreement, and said, 'I suppose opening the crypt won't be any more pleasant.'

'Probably not. Opening old graves doesn't lend itself to – well – pleasure.'

She rose, went to the packages and took

them back to him. 'Go and see if they fit.'

He didn't argue, and after he'd gone into another room she returned to the locket, carrying it to the doorway where sunlight brightened the portrait. Angelina Montoya had been a classical beauty, delicate, almost fragile with those great dark eyes dominating her otherwise perfect features. The unknown artist had been very good; he'd captured a look in the eyes that seemed not so much sad and wise, as haunted, although there was something of sad wisdom in the face too. It was almost as though murdered Angelina Montoya was begging Dolores to intercede for her.

She closed the locket with a little shudder, put it back on the table and turned when Whitney re-entered the room, faintly smiling. The suit, of excellent tropical cloth, fitted perfectly. Even the shirt and tie were exactly right for him.

'Your uncle,' he said, 'is a very observant man. We only met once but he remembered very well.'

'You look very handsome,' said Dolores, speaking candidly. 'You also need a haircut.'

He laughed. 'I can take care of that myself.'

She nodded. 'I'll meet you at the cannon tomorrow afternoon.'

'Do you have to go now?'

'Yes.'

'Are we agreed? Neither of us will mention Angelina?'

She nodded, letting her gaze stray back to the locket. 'I wish I knew who she was.'

'By tomorrow afternoon I'll be able to tell you,' he said, going out into the sunlight with her, towards the drowsing horse. 'I know most of the natives who live along the shore. I can find out without arousing wonder, I suppose. They love to talk anyway. But don't you ask.'

'I won't.' She turned with the reins in her hand. 'I wish we hadn't dug her up though.'

He was fatalistic. 'But we did, and I suppose whatever her secret was is now our secret too.'

'Do you think there could be danger, Whitney?'

He didn't see how. 'After all, she's been dead a very long time. Even if her murderer might have killed again to protect himself, he's been dead a long while by now himself. No, I don't think there's much danger. Probably none at all, but on the other hand I do think discretion on our part is wisest.'

He touched her cheek gently. His hand was rough but the movement was tender. He smiled at her. She didn't feel very brave right at that moment and he seemed to realize it.

He bent, lightly brushed her lips with his mouth, then reached past to hold the horse while she mounted. It had been a natural thing between them, her uneasiness, his move to reassure her. She evened-up the reins, looked at him and said, 'You were going to tell me something afterwards, weren't you?'

He understood and gazed up at her for a moment before speaking. 'I haven't mentioned it before.'

She touched his hand where it lay upon the horse's neck. 'Today is my day for keeping secrets.'

'It isn't that, entirely. I just haven't wanted to mention it before. But five years have passed... My wife and I came here from Cuba, escaping from the island in the night. We almost made it too, but a Cuban patrol craft sighted us, gave chase and machine-gunned our boat... My wife was killed, I was wounded – not badly except for the loss of blood. Then we escaped when nightfall fell again. But she was dead and the boat was leaking badly. I plugged the holes as best I could, reached this beach, buried her that same night, took the boat out to deep water, sunk it and swam back. After that, I lay in this cottage, which was a roofless ruin then, scarcely moving for several days. I don't know how long. Gradually, after-wards, I recovered and – well – just stayed on. That's the whole story.'

Dolores said softly, 'I'm terribly sorry, Whitney.'

He smiled up at her. 'You'd better go. I'll be waiting by the Three Sisters tomorrow at sunset.'

'The Three Sisters?'

'That what the natives call the three little bronze cannon. It's the Spanish way; they show affection for inanimate things that have served them well.'

'Oh. I'll be along about five, I suppose. Goodbye.'

He stepped back for the horse to turn, watched her out of sight, and when she topped out upon the higher ground and paused to glance back, he was no longer in sight.

There were shadows down by the cottage now, cool and vague, while up where she sat on the horse, sunshine lay as always, humidly bright and golden. She unconsciously glanced off in the direction of the grave they'd opened, then feeling an unnatural little chill, she turned the horse and spurred it into a gallop up where the heat was, for once, very welcome.

At the stable old Gregorio was waiting, broad smile splitting his wrinkled old mahogany face. She had to smile back but it was an effort, and when he took the horse saying unless she hastened she'd be late for supper, she didn't argue with him although he had previously impressed upon her the Spanish tradition of each rider looking after his – or her – mount.

At the house, her uncle had just returned from the fields. She heard him in his rooms as she passed down the cool hall to her own quarters. It was a very reassuring sound, too, those masculine noises.

She bathed, changed, then stood by an open window listening to the parrots in the tall trees, seeing the orderly rows of citrus trees in the near distance, hearing the soft lowing of distant cattle, and catching sight of the first faint spirals of smoke coming from beyond sight where the workers were ending their day too, and their wives were preparing dinner.

Nothing was changed. Everything she'd

grown accustomed to since her arrival at Estate Sao Paolo looked the same. And yet nothing really was the same because in the forefront of her thoughts loomed that delicate, beautiful face with its sad-haunted dark eyes.

She turned and resolutely left the room to go to dinner, and although the temptation was very strong, when she saw her uncle and he greeted her with admiring eyes, she made no mention of Angelina Montoya, who had been shot dead then hurriedly wrapped in cloth and dumped into a shallow grave.

Chapter Seven

A LONG DAY OF WAITING

The day of the party began like almost any other day at Estate Sao Paolo. Hernan' came for his *patron* in the battered Land Rover, but instead of arriving alone, today he brought four women with him, wives of the men. They would help at the house preparing food, cleaning and dusting, washing down the stone patios, in general, doing domestic chores.

Dolores went out to the Land Rover with her uncle. He would be in one of the pastures until about noon, he said, and afterwards would return to take a nap and get ready for the reception.

He also thought it might not be a bad idea if she stuck close to the *hacienda* to make certain the women set things in proper order. He laughed and winked as he said that. 'Someday you'll be a housewife; after all you can't spend your entire life riding horses.' He climbed into the little vehicle beside grinning Hernan' Godoy, and drove away.

She inhaled deeply. The morning was azure, fragrant, serene and cool. A splendid day to go for a ride. Watching the Land Rover scuff dust, she shrugged and returned to the house. Of course her uncle was right, but then she'd never thought otherwise. Someday she would marry. As for riding horses, she was certain that pleasure would always remain with her, but it need not interfere with other things. Men! Single-track minds!

The women were gabbling in their own peculiar variety of *patois* Spanish. Dolores got the gist of their talk without actually understanding very many of the words.

They smiled at her, showed some defer-ence, and were very busy as long as she was in sight. The cook, who was always in the house, had taken charge. She showed an attitude of genteel superiority which fitted her well and which the other women did not appear to resent.

Actually, there was very little for Dolores to do. She would be responsible for proper place settings later, when the Irish linen was brought forth for the buffet tables, and also for other final arrangements, but as the gabbling and bustle increased, she escaped to the barn where at least it was quiet and peaceful.

Gregorio was soaping leather, examining plaited reins, muttering to himself about how hostile humid weather was to leather. He didn't hear Dolores until she stepped on to the gravel out front, put there to prevent mud from making a quagmire round the stables during the rainy season.

He turned, squinted from beneath his floppy-brimmed old hat, then smiled widely. '*Señorita,* tonight is the fine *fandango,* no?'

She smiled, nodded and watched his claw-like old mahogany hands caress the leather. It was blessedly cool in the little breeze-way where they stood. He continued to smile and went back to his work with the leather.

'When I was a young man … it was a long time ago … my country was a place of great celebrations, great *fandangos*. Of course I left before those *barbudos* – those bearded ones people call the *Fidelistas* – took over the government, so of course I know nothing of the changes. Well, at least I only know what I hear. But in my youth Cuba was a splendid place. Not rich; whoever is rich anyway? But we fished a lot, you understand, *Señorita*, and danced by moonlight, and made love, and worked hard when the cane was ready. Well, it was a good life.' The old face lifted and turned. '*Mi patron Don Francisco Montoya* came to me one day and said, Gregorio, I want you to go to my land in Puerto Rico as *mayor domo* and see why it is that the cattle die, the cane does not ever make a crop, and to help my family in that place.

'So I came here, *Señorita,* and that was a great many years ago, and after a while I went down to live in the village. A man, when he ages, is entitled to sit in the shade, no?'

Dolores was gazing at the old man with a strange intensity. When he paused in his ramblings to turn and smile, she said, 'Did your *patron* come here too, Gregorio?'

'*Don Francisco?*' he said looking surprised. 'Oh no, *Señorita.* He was a very rich and powerful man in Cuba, and men like that dare not leave, even for a short while. If they do, then when they return someone else has taken everything. No, *mi patron* – may he rest in peace – died three years later – although actually not an old man at all – and I never saw him again.'

Dolores was poised with her next question when the sound of a car down by the house distracted her. Old Gregorio stepped past, peered, stepped back and said, '*El patron, Señorita,* has now returned from the fields.' He grinned at her. 'I had never worked for a *Norte Americano,* so when I heard he needed a man with the horses, well, I had been retired long enough so I came and got this work. But until you came I was thinking of retiring again. These *paisanos* are all farmers, who work for your uncle, and we of the old ways, well, we are very proud of our horsemanship. There is a difference, no?'

She rose, smiled and said, 'There is a difference, yes,' and strolled out of the stable in time to see her uncle and his overseer carrying enormous armloads of exotic flowers into the house. That, naturally, would fall into her realm, the arranging and positioning of the bouquets, so she hastened on down to the house with only a mental note to encourage Gregorio to tell more of his connection with a family named Montoya.

The morning came and went, the afternoon seemed to hasten along. The cleaning-women finished their work, and the cook herded them into her private domain and mildly bullied them into helping with the preparations which were required in that area. Howard Fitzgerald took Dolores out on to the rear patio where they both had a cold drink in the humid shade, and he grinned a little ruefully when he confided that although he had had other gatherings at the villa since acquiring it, they had always been small, and with very few women on hand. He wasn't nervous, he said, but was not quite able to predict how things would go, and that, his disposition being what it was, caused him concern. He offered a personal maxim.

'Never go into a meeting or attend a party, never plan a campaign nor order work, without doing your utmost to control the final results.'

She had to smile. The rules of business were hardly applicable now. She said, 'I didn't believe I'd ever see you worried, Uncle Howard. Don't worry, you told me just the other night that people are the same. The party will be a success. It could scarcely be otherwise with Rosaria Aldama, could it?'

'Well, with Rosaria, certainly it will be a success from the masculine standpoint. But you too, are very lovely. But then you'd know that.'

She liked his admiration, which had been evident the first time he'd set his eyes upon her. But she did not now, never had, considered herself beautiful. Strong and adaptable, fair and attractive, yes, but not beautiful. She shook her head, thinking of Rosaria's *real* beauty, but before she could speak again, her uncle took a fresh tack on another topic.

'You haven't told me whether the clothes fit.'

'Perfectly. He put them on and looked very aristocratic in them.'

'He wasn't angry?'

'He said he would pay for them.'

'I see. Well, for your sake I hope he fits in.'

She was confident. 'He'll belong. No matter who the others are, he'll adapt very well.'

Her uncle finished his drink, put the glass

down and turned to study her. 'You aren't becoming *too* interested, are you?'

She was cool with her answer. 'Don't you think I should?'

He side-stepped the pit she'd left open for him by simply saying 'I don't know, Dee. I have a world of faith in your judgement. Still, we don't know much about him, do we?'

'Enough, I think, Uncle Howard.'

His brows climbed. 'Oh…?"

'He is a widower. His wife was killed when they were fleeing Cuba in a motor-boat. He buried her down there by the cottage.'

'I see.'

'He is gentle and kindly, with a good sense of humour, Uncle Howard. If you knew him I'm certain you would like him.'

'Probably.' He glanced at his wrist. 'If I'm to stay up most of the night, love, I'd better take a nap now.' He grinned. 'Old bones, you know. By the way, I presume you'll be driving down for him.'

'Yes. To the *castella*. He'll walk up there

from his cottage.'

'You'd better scoot along then.' He hesitated, looking at her. Finally he quietly said, 'Dolores, please be careful. Your father would not like it if anything happened while you were down there. He'd blame me.'

She smiled. He was a decent man, kindly and understanding. As a parent he'd have been a little overly protective, perhaps. She stepped in close, raised up and planted a kiss on his cheek. 'I won't do anything to upset my father … or you, Uncle Howard. Goodbye; I'll be back with him in an hour or so. Have a good nap.'

She waited until he'd gone into the house, wondering whether to change from her sandals, jeans and blouse *before* she went after Whitney, or after they returned. She decided to wait until they returned, went out where two Land Rovers stood in the shade of a giant catalpa whose cabbage-sized flowers dropped little pink and white petals, took the vehicle which looked cleanest, and drove off through the lengthening shadows along one of the narrow roads that skirted planted fields, forming little dusty ribbons between jungle and cultivated land.

The parrots were beginning to seek perches, birds of different varieties, including shiny black crows who were just as raucous as parrots, rose by the score from the groves, winging towards the darker green of the natural covert.

The dust had a coppery scent, faint though noticeable, and reddish sunlight reflecting off the Land Rover's bonnet was like aerated rust.

She had to slow once for some kind of fat, furry large animal to waddle with ungainly haste across the road into the jungle. She had no idea what the beast was, but Whitney would know, if she remembered to ask. There was something else making her hasten. He would also have the answer to what was more firmly uppermost in her thoughts. At least he'd seemed very positive he'd have that answer when she'd left him the day before.

She reached the promontory almost a full hour early. He wasn't there and she hadn't expected him to be. It was a delightful spot, actually. She left the car, went over to stand by the Three Sisters, and feel again that glass-smooth metal warmth. She stepped behind the little cannons and bent to sight out to sea. Evidently, when the guns had been placed there, whoever had been the overseer had decided to have the muzzles cover a particular square of deep water, as though he knew the pirates would always have to approach from a certain direction. It was highly probable that was the only deep-water channel, out there, near enough to the shore to facilitate black-powder cannon-ades.

It was so peaceful now, so empty and endless, it was difficult to imagine anyone ever sweeping along with great sails billowing, bent on murder and pillage.

The bougainvillaea vine, with its blood-red flowers dropping velvet petals all around the little guns, and a central bole as thick as a man's wrist; it had to be a very old plant, probably hand-planted in this spot since it was the only such plant anywhere in sight, and she leaned in the wonderful ebbing day wondering about that too.

Puerto Rico was old, its history spotted, colourful, full of improbable legends, some bold, some tender, all fascinating to someone whose own personal world had a very practical, pragmatic kind of history.

She turned from the sea, sighted movement along the lower-down path, and left the Three Sisters to go and greet Whitney as he came striding along.

He threw her a kiss from three hundred feet, white teeth showing in the darkness of his face. She threw one back without a thought.

He came on up, scarcely breathing hard from the climb, and said, 'How beautiful you are, my Lady of the Forest.'

She blushed in spite of herself. 'In these old clothes? Whitney, you got a haircut. That must amount to a small miracle, here along the beach.'

'Not really. I have friends among the fishermen and wood cutters. I spent most of the night down the coast a couple of miles in their village.'

She let the smile fade. 'And…?'

'Do you really want to know?'

'Is it that bad, Whitney?'

'In a way, perhaps. But it's history so there's nothing left of it but the story – and the forlorn grave.' He brought the locket forth from a pocket. He had polished it to its original high shine. 'It belongs to you,' he said, pushing it into her hand. 'I didn't bring the bracelet or brooch. You'll have them too, but you'll have to visit me again to get them. That's how I make sure you'll come.'

She held the locket and didn't look at him as she said, 'I'd have come anyway. You know that.'

He took her hand, led her to the car, leaned her there and said, 'Now, or later?'

'Now, please.'

Chapter Eight

A HECTIC DAY

First, he cautioned her by saying something to the effect that Spanish as well as native imaginations were inclined to be romantic; when tales were told it was almost obligatory for the teller to add colour, to heighten the drama, to prove himself worthy.

'Angelina Montoya was the only daughter of a man named Francisco Montoya.'

'A Cuban,' she said quietly. 'Very wealthy, who owned land here and in Cuba also.'

Whitney stopped, looked at her hard, then said, 'I thought you weren't going to ask around.'

'I didn't. My uncle's stableman, old Gregorio, got to rambling on this morning. He told me a Cuban named Francisco

Montoya had sent him here to Puerto Rico when Gregorio was a young man. I wouldn't even like to guess Gregorio's age now, but it would be well up there.'

'I see. You picked up the name.'

'Yes. But that's all.'

'Well, *your* Francisco Montoya was a descendant of Angelina, but *his* father had the same name. In any event, Angelina came here to visit a family of wealth and breeding who owned an adjoining plantation – next to the Montoya holdings. She was to marry the son of the other family. She disappeared. It was rumoured that she'd run off with a *Yanqui* gunrunner who was selling weapons to Cuban insurgents. But no one was ever sure of that. All anyone ever knew what that she disappeared.'

When Whitney stopped speaking Dolores gazed up at him. 'Who did it?'

He shrugged. 'Young Francisco Montoya, is my guess. You see, there is another bit of ancient gossip that has her, in fact, actually meeting and falling in love with this *Yanqui* gunrunner. *That* story, not generally told any more, says Francisco followed her one night after a great ball at the Estate Sao Paolo, found her in the arms of the gunrunner, and shot them both.'

'But – you said Francisco was her brother. Wouldn't it be more logical for the man she was to have married to have done that?'

'Nowadays, perhaps, but Angelina died one hundred and ten years ago. That was when she disappeared. In those days there was Spanish honour. A brother, finding his own sister having an affair with another man although already promised – and that lover being a *Yanqui,* in those days not much different from the devil himself – would think of his family's pride first. At least that's how I've analysed it.'

'And the gunrunner?'

'I don't know. The two tales get pretty well romanticized after that. One says he sailed away with the exquisite Angelina and they lived happily forever after. The natural conclusion to such a legend, I suppose. The other story, not so well known, stops right after Francisco Montoya, who was *patron* of Estate Sao Paolo at that time, supposedly put a bullet into his sister's head.'

Dolores said softly, 'Gregorio says *his* Francisco Montoya – who would be either the son or grandson of the murderer – died while still not an old man. Lord, what a terrible thing to have to live with.'

Whitney stood watching Dolores thoughtfully. Finally he said, 'Well, according to my calculations, Francisco couldn't have been terribly young when he died. After all Angelina died a hundred and ten years ago.'

'It would have been impossible,' said Dolores, then, with a fresh idea, spoke on. 'Do you suppose the man who killed Angelina could have been the *father* of Gregorio's *Don* Francisco?'

'That would fit. As for your old stableman, granting he may be having some of the initial difficulties of senility, he nevertheless may still be able to give us more information. Anyway, we're only jumping to a conclusion about which Francisco killed Angelina, aren't we?'

'Yes, it certainly seems so.' Dolores straightened up off the car, turned and strolled across to the little cannons, put a hand out and stood there for a moment with her back to Whitney. 'It's so sad,' she said.

He agreed. He also touched upon something that was actually closer to what was troubling her than the fact of an old murder. 'We found her yesterday. Today, we have some of the story. It makes it seem as though we knew her; as though a full century hasn't passed at all.'

She turned. 'Whitney, whatever became of the man who loved her?'

'He married, had children, died and his grandson married a very lovely woman: Rosaria Aldama.'

She was astonished. 'Aldama…? I had no idea…' She kept looking at Whitney. 'I know Rosaria. At least I've met her. Now it makes the thing seem even closer, more personal.'

He didn't speak although he kept gazing at

her, and meanwhile the sun began to drop down towards that blue-green slot of distant sea where it sank each day.

She came out of her shock looking and feeling a little sad, a little forlorn. She had only that fragile portrait to link her with a beautiful girl who had died violently because of a misplaced love, but somehow, just holding the golden locket in her hand made Angelina seem so close and believable.

'Maybe we'd better go along,' he murmured. 'I'm sorry I told you.'

She smiled at him. 'I'm glad. Otherwise I'd have lain awake every night for the rest of my visit.'

She had not mentioned before that she would not be here much longer. He forgot Angelina at once as he climbed in beside her and said, 'How much longer will you be here?'

'Two weeks.' She started the car, backed around, set it towards home and ran through the gears but without speed. She looked at him, saw something in his profile and said, 'I should have explained about that before. I'm sorry, Whitney.'

'Two weeks is a lifetime, Dolores.' He was smiling again, not with the same old spontaneity, but smiling nonetheless.

She reverted to the other thing. 'What a dreadful thing for Francisco Montoya to do. His own sister.'

'I think I explained that. At any rate I can tell you from personal experience that honour is a tremendous thing even yet among the oldest, proudest Spanish families in this part of the world.'

'But … to *kill* her…'

He was quiet for a while, until they were passing down along the jungle, with the orderly citrus rows on their left. 'Well, I'm afraid it happened pretty much as we now understand it.'

'Rosaria would probably know something.'

He gave her an odd look. 'Would it be very wise, asking? I mean, surely within the old families they would know what really happened, but no one would care much about having it brought out again.'

'But you said Rosaria married an Aldama. That doesn't make *her* one.'

He reached, lay a hand upon her arm and said, 'Rosaria's maiden name was Montoya.'

Dolores gave a little start. Then she said, 'Of course. I should have guessed it. She used to live at Estate Sao Paolo. I think someone told me that. Either that she lived here or her family did. But if the place belonged to ... did they sell it, Whitney, after the tragedy?'

He didn't know. He hadn't asked any such question among the people he'd gone to visit the night before. All he said was the same thing he'd mentioned moments earlier.

'I don't think it will help anyone, certainly not poor Angelina, if you ask Rosaria, or any of the other local aristocracy, about that old murder.'

Of course he was perfectly correct. She

drove along turning the entire bizarre situation over in her mind. Not only was he correct, he was also proving to be both wise and gifted with a penetrating sagacity. She looked at him. He was turned away, watching the even-spaced rows of citrus trees whip past. His profile showed a stony, settled kind of sadness. She had not seen him look this way before.

They came within sight of the villa. Rosaria's low-slung, sleek foreign car was out front, as were several other vehicles. Dolores mumbled something about having no idea they'd taken so long getting back. She still had to bathe and get freshly dressed.

They drove round back where the Land Rover belonged, got out and she took him through the kitchen and pantry to the front of the house. There, she caught her uncle's eye and asked him to introduce Whitney around until she returned. She then fled to her own quarters, flung clothes aside in a great rush and went through the work of getting herself prepared for the first party she'd attended in Puerto Rico.

She had some difficulty clearing her mind of the Angelina Montoya matter, and she had one advantage over Whitney Jackson in that regard; *she'd* only seen the Angelina preserved in that locket. He had seen a quite different, contemporary Angelina. When she thought of the affair at all she easily conjured up the beautiful face with those enormous dark and pleading eyes.

One of the servants came to say the people were going to the buffet now to eat, and her uncle wondered if she hadn't better hasten. She called from the dressing-table saying she would be right along, then forced herself to take more time at putting on a fresh face.

Finally, when she was ready, a last critical look in the wall-mirror showed a tallish girl with short, curly brown hair and level blue eyes whose skin – face, throat, shoulders, upper arms – was a shade of gold-tan, and whose features were strong, even handsome, but different altogether from the local variety of beauty. Fairer, sturdier, somehow more robust-seeming, Rosaria Aldama, for example, had the transparent beauty of a frail woman. She did not give an impression of being very frail, but her beauty was not the kind one usually associated with tomboys, horsewomen, self-reliant and capable females, while Dolores Harper's beauty was precisely this kind.

She shrugged bare, rounded shoulders. A woman could do the best with what the beauty-aid industry produced, and beyond that she could do very little, and if she happened not to actually care too much about her beauty, that is, she accepted it as a natural endowment and did not spend most of her waking hours seeking to enhance it, then she emerged as that most rare of all females, the natural beauty.

She left the room, went quickly through to the dining-room, and was immediately seen by Rosaria who took her in hand and started around introducing her to people.

The dining-room, although of fair dimensions, was full. Not knowing many of her uncle's guests nearly kept her from getting anything to eat and she was famished. By the time Rosaria had completed the introductions most of the guests were already seated, eating, conversing, laughing, waving back and forth.

Her uncle was with John Gore, the grey and distinguished-looking former governor. Frederick Gore, the son, was seeing to the seating of his mother, a somewhat rawboned, leathery woman to whom a combination of tropics and age had not been very kind.

Whitney appeared with a laden plate. He pointed and led her towards a place at one of the tables where two people could sit, and afterwards he leaned, brushing her bare shoulder, to say. 'I wanted to tell you something this evening – some time – and I'm sure this isn't the moment, but every time I see Frederick Gore looking at you, I feel a need for urgency.' He brushed her ear with his lips. 'I'm in love with you.' He straightened up and quietly started eating.

And of course he had been right; Frederick Gore strode over, edged in on the far side of Dolores, turned large, sultry eyes upon Dolores and said, 'Did you know we'd already heard of you down at San Juan? News of great beauty covers this island within days. And you *are* very lovely.'

She met his smile with one equally as polite but a lot less fervent. 'I doubt if there has been anyone in Puerto Rico for a great many years who could be compared in beauty with Rosaria Aldama.'

Frederick kept smiling. 'But she's *old* and you are *young*. It's the difference between freshness and preserved beauty. You see, I'm an amateur authority; I've made quite a study of beauty. So when I say you are stunning, you must believe me.'

He was persistent but she was still hungry. She returned to her meal conscious of his eyes rarely leaving her. After a while it annoyed her, but she stifled the irritation,

telling herself that manners in Puerto Rico
were quite different from masculine manners in New England.

Chapter Nine

NIGHT OF THE PARTY

In New England where there was more natural reserve, putting together a successful party required real talent. In Puerto Rico although the upper-class did not fraternize with the lower-class, the easy familiarity and good-natured amiability of the peasant infiltrated the atmosphere of the wealthy making the island famous for the pleasure of its parties as well as for the geniality of its heterogenous people.

Dolores enjoyed the people; they were helpful, very pleasant to her, and willing to go out of their way to show her the island. The only one who made that offer with ulterior motives was Frederick Gore and she put him off with a smile – and a quick return of her irritation. She told Whitney Jackson that if she were a man she'd punch Fred Gore right in the nose, and for some reason that made Whitney laugh up-roariously.

Rosaria, in a white dress that set off her exquisite beauty and golden skin to perfection, caught Dolores and Whitney out upon the patio watching a moon work through some tufted little transparent clouds, and said there was only one man in the entire group she'd like to have corner her, and he was the only one who didn't make the effort.

Dolores smiled. She had an idea who that one man was; she'd seen the way Rosaria Aldama looked at her uncle. Whitney offered to get them both a glass of iced punch, and went off.

Rosaria smiled. 'You look happy,' she said. 'When I was your age each new moon was pure silver and each young man was Prince Charming.'

Dolores became conscious of something

that was revealed in moonlight and which had not been noticeable at all in the house. Rosaria resembled Angelina Montoya. Even the white dress, the sleek mass of ebony hair, the large, liquid eyes lifted now towards those tufted clouds. It was an uncanny sensation.

Dolores said, 'Rosaria, you said your husband's family were the founders of Estate Sao Paolo...'

She dropped her eyes and turned. 'No, not the founders. At least if I said that it was a mistake. No one knows who initially cleared the jungle for the house. The Aldama family were among the earliest owners. But then so were the Montoyas.'

'The Montoyas?'

'My family, Dolores. Montoya is my maiden name. The Montoyas came along later though, after the Aldama family had sold Sao Paolo and moved over to the plantation where I live now. That great-grandmother I told you about, the one who comes to all the parties at Sao Paolo, she was an Aldama.' Rosaria smiled. 'I haven't seen her tonight, though. Well, she would be several hundred years old by now and the elderly need their rest, eh?'

Dolores wanted to keep Rosaria talking but Whitney returned with their spiked punch. He said Frank McFall, whom Dolores remembered as being burly and aggressive, was telling jokes, and they were actually very funny. He seemed surprised; evidently he'd appraised McFall as quite different.

Rosaria could enlighten them both. 'He is very competitive, but that's his nature and the Lord knows Puerto Rico needs some of that. We've been living with the feudal system too long as it is. Frank asked me to marry him last summer.' Rosaria's golden eyes sparkled. 'It was very good for my ego. He is an energetic, sometimes abrasive person, but very successful. On our island success is almost a religion.'

Whitney made a remark to which Dolores at once attached special meaning. He said, 'I suppose in the early days success was perpetuated by intermarriage among the old, wealthy families.'

Rosaria looked at him and nodded. 'That's been universal, though. In Europe it was the same. Still is, I think, whenever one rich family can find another with an eligible child.' She turned, as though wearying of the conversation, looked through the lighted doorway and smiled. People were mingling, and there was music. She turned back towards Dolores. 'Do you like to dance?'

Dolores nodded.

Rosaria smiled and winked. 'I love to.'

She left them, going back indoors, and the night became different, less wise and less dazzling; more serene and quietly pensive.

Dolores said, 'She didn't draw out very well did she? I mean, when you led her on with that question of oldtime marriages.'

He grinned. 'I'm not a very good interrogator. But I'm not sure just what I'm looking for either.'

'Verification of the legends?'

'Possibly. But which legend?'

Dolores was practical. 'The true one.'

He said, 'I think we know which is the true one. We know Angelina didn't sail away with her buccaneer.'

He could have mentioned the bullethole too, but he did not. It wasn't necessary; Angelina had never left the island. That was quite enough to know.

Dolores looked out where pewter moonlight shone upon rank after rank of planted trees. She was remembering something he'd leaned to whisper in her ear at dinner, and somehow it was mixed up with the affair of Angelina, making a very bizarre situation.

He touched her. 'If you really like to dance...'

They went back indoors and met her uncle who had just left a group of his guests and was moving towards the next group. He winked at her. 'Going rather well,' he confided.

She smiled. 'I told you it would. By the

way – have you danced with Rosaria yet?'

He shook his head, eyeing her brightly. 'Should I?'

He was teasing her and she knew it. 'If you don't, Uncle Howard, I'm afraid Whitney will. I'd just as soon he didn't.'

The men both blinked.

She took them both by the arm and led the way towards the dancing. She saw burly, short Frank McFall eyeing them and smiled. He smiled back.

The former governor's wife, Alice Gore, was standing along the wall watching the dancers. On the spur of the moment Dolores halted her uncle directly in front of the angular, faded woman. He took the hint perfectly.

Whitney stepped aside for the others to move out and leaned as he did so, to say, 'Your adoring Fred Gore may feel Rosaria is too old, but I get the impression he believes in any port in a storm.'

The younger Gore was dancing with Rosaria.

The music was Latin by almost any standards, but it also showed some calypso influence, making it irresistible to anyone at all who possessed a sense of rhythm. Dolores turned and Whitney was there waiting.

He said, 'I haven't seen Morrison.'

Her uncle's secretary had been gone for ten days. In fact, she'd only just met him when he'd had to go to the mainland on business for his employer. She said something to that effect, then saw Frederick Gore watching her and managed to turn her partner without seeming to do so, thus presenting her back to young Gore. It may have been a casual rebuff but he kept staring.

When the music stopped her uncle came over to say Mrs Gore was a surprisingly good dancer. Remembering what Whitney had remarked about, she asked about Morrison. Her uncle was offhand in his answer.

'He'll be back within a day or two. There

were some things needing care of in New York.' He then turned to Whitney and said, 'I'm not a very good neighbour, but I've built a kind of rigorous routine for myself here. I apologize though for not riding down.'

Whitney's easy poise was equal to this occasion. 'It's been my fault more than yours, but I suppose men are more likely to create private worlds than women.'

Her uncle studied the tanned, strong, younger face as he nodded slowly. 'I want you to come back though,' he said with unsmiling sincerity. 'Having Dolores here is like re-living my youth, but as you suggested, men need more.' He smiled and turned as Rosaria came over. The music was starting again. The two of them moved away.

Whitney stood a moment watching, then Dolores captured his attention by saying, 'I thought she might be coming for you.'

He shook his head. 'There would be no question of choice between your uncle and me, where Rosaria Aldama is concerned.'

She looked up swiftly. Something in the way he'd said that struck a chord deep inside her. He was still watching the dancers so she also turned to watch.

Her uncle was holding Rosaria without stiffness, and she clung to him with a calm gentleness. They did not say much, which was different from most of the other dancing couples. They danced very well together.

Dolores, succumbing to an earlier impression, said, 'She is so beautiful I don't see how he's kept away from her.'

Whitney looked down. 'He hasn't, love.'

'What do you mean?'

'Nothing. They see each other frequently. It's no great secret. They've been seeing each other for several years. You're new here or you'd have noticed it. Personally, I think it's a good thing.'

She said, 'Do you get all this from your fishermen-friends?'

He smiled. 'Some of it. But I've seen them

together down along the seashore.'

'He's only mentioned her as a neighbour,' said Dolores, still watching the dancing couple. 'If he's known her all these years, and if they've been friendly...' She raised her face and found him smiling at her. 'Well...?'

'I'm sure I can't answer that. But I suppose being a little older they're in no hurry. Anyway, it could just be friendship, couldn't it?'

She nodded without actually believing it could be just friendship. Her uncle was lean and handsome and wealthy. Rosaria, also wealthy, was additionally very beautiful. She didn't think age could have much to do with it.

'Cold Yankee blood,' he laughed. 'Would you care to dance?'

As she went up against him she said, 'Whitney, does Rosaria remind you of anyone?'

He caught the innuendo immediately. 'Yes, but, after all, they are of the same family, and there hasn't been so many generations between them. Then too, there is the identical colouring. Rosaria has lighter eyes than Angelina, but her hair, her features, her *kind* of beauty is the same.'

'I wish we dared ask her.'

'In time we probably will get the chance, although as I said earlier, I'm not at all sure it's a wise course.'

She suddenly thought of something and looked up. 'Old Gregorio. We could ask *him*.'

He was about to reply when Fred Gore came towards them. She saw his approach from the corner of her eye and clung tighter to Whitney, but it was permissible for a male to cut in, so when Fred's leering smile appeared over her shoulder, Whitney tactfully if not with any show of enthusiasm, relinquished his hold.

Gore was a good dancer, but then his kind usually was. Also, he had an agreeable patter ranging from the weather to her fresh beauty. She could have closed her eyes and imagined herself dancing with any one of a number of men she had encountered since graduating from college, and even before that, while still in college.

He made no advances although he verbally laid all the proper groundwork for doing so later. Only once did he capture her attention. That was when he said, 'Rosaria told me you and Whitney Jackson are old friends.'

There was, of course, something behind that statement, since Gore had to know she'd only been a guest of her uncle for a couple of weeks. She said, 'Is that so?' and coolly waited for him to elaborate. He never did, although he enigmatically smiled throughout the rest of their dance, until she could have slapped his face.

Later, she told Whitney, and was thoughtful, but it was difficult to be alone as the evening ran on. She had to dance with John Gore, Fred's father. Then she was cornered by Frank McFall, who turned out to be very interesting. He missed nothing and knew a good deal of local gossip. She could tell that he also knew something about her uncle and Rosaria Aldama because, although he kept her interest by ticking off amusing anecdotes about everyone else at the party, he never once mentioned Rosaria or Howard Fitzgerald.

There were other men, too, who claimed her for dances, but they were simply faces attached to names she remembered. Even the curate, Father Alfonso Cordoba, danced with her, and although she'd never before danced with a priest, wasn't even sure they were supposed to do such things as attend dances, he turned out to be very pleasant and possessed of a delightful sense of humour. He confided to her that Latin American priests were very rare birds indeed, which was in fact a very interesting truth.

Chapter Ten

A KISS – AND A MURDER

Alice and John Gore were the first to leave. It was then well past midnight. Whitney said he would walk home, that it was a beautiful night and he liked hiking. Dolores wouldn't hear of it. She ran to tell her uncle she would be gone a while, driving him back to the promontory, and then she took him by the hand out to the same Land Rover she'd used in fetching him. He even suggested taking the car and driving himself home, then returning it in the morning. She did not accede to that either.

'You can't just run off,' he protested. 'The party was in your honour.'

She said she would be back before the other guests departed, punched the starter-button and swung the rough-riding little vehicle away from the lighted hacienda towards the dark and distant highlands that rose steadily but gently towards the distant *castella barranca.*

He was quiet most of the way, and once when she looked over, he was pulling off his tie, opening the throat of his shirt. She smiled at that; she had never before seen him wearing a tie, or any other kind of attire that constricted movement. It was easy to imagine he felt much more free and comfortable the way he sat now, watching the jungle spin past on one side, the citrus rows on the opposite side.

There was no noise other than that made by the Land Rover. For once the gaudy parrots were silent. When she passed the place where she'd encountered that ungainly, furry beast earlier, she remembered, but didn't bother his thoughtful solitude by asking what it might have been. It wasn't important. Neither, she told herself with much less conviction, was that innuendo of Fred Gore's about she and Whitney Jackson being old friends. What Gore had been hinting was that she and Whitney were *intimate* friends. She gripped the wheel hard thinking again that she'd liked to have slapped Gore's face.

He said suddenly, 'It was a very pleasant gathering. I enjoyed it.'

She wasn't so sure she had. 'Really, Whitney?'

'Really. And you were the most beautiful woman there. It made me proud of you.'

She looked over. 'Rosaria…?'

'You were still the most beautiful.'

They smiled at one another. Then the land began its slight lift and on ahead moonlight shone off the wind-scourged barren acre or two of land where the little cannon kept their eternal vigil. She slowed for the last hundred yards because the road up here, with less need for attention, got less of it.

Then they shot out into the open, stopped, and down below the endless stirring of the sea rolling along the base of the granite cliff was softly audible. She turned as though to alight. He caught her arm, pulled her gently back around and reached to lift her face. She did not resist.

When their lips met he was tender. A tiny explosion occurred somewhere in her breast and she lifted both arms to his shoulders.

Then they parted and instead of looking away, she smiled. 'That was very sweet. Very platonic.'

He blinked. 'It wasn't meant to be – platonic.'

'Well, I'm sorry. That wasn't just the word I wanted.'

He kissed her again, and if she could feel his needs and hungers this time, he could also feel her quick and sturdy response.

That time when they parted she *did* avoid his eyes. She swung clear, got out of the car and walked slowly up where the crumbling old stone wall prevented inadvertent falling down the sheer cliff-face.

He followed her, leaving his coat behind in the car, looking dark and handsome and strong in the moonlight.

'Usually,' he said, gazing out to sea and sounding as though there was nothing between them, 'you can see the lights of ships out there. Excursion boats from Florida or up along the Eastern Seaboard.'

She said, 'Which did you originally sail from, Whitney?'

He didn't baulk; he may even have expected something like this. 'Neither, actually. I came down from Mexico.' When she turned he smiled. 'That only makes it more than ever mysterious, I know. But it's really not. I represented a major oil company. I had the Caribbean area – quite large territory in a matter of miles. Then I took full charge in Cuba. You can guess the rest. The revolution came, I tried to flee … I told you what happened.'

'But, didn't you want to go back to the States?'

He watched the soft-heaving sea and shook his head. 'What for? My wife was the only reason I ever struggled anyway. There was enough money, otherwise.'

'You loved her?'

'Yes. But now I'm glad there were no children.' He looked at her. 'Five years is long enough to be alone, Dolores. Too long, actually.'

'Whitney? Would she…?'

'Haunt us? No. She was good to me. I'll always remember the good times. I'm trying to be very honest with you. I've wrestled it out with myself these past couple of weeks trying to be honest with myself, and with her memory too. But she *isn't*, Dolores, and I *am* – and you *are*.'

He didn't try to explain that. It wasn't necessary in any case. She nodded and turned to also watch the heavy-heaving sea. 'I don't know what to say, Whitney. I … It just never entered my mind when I got off the airplane at San Juan.'

He touched her profiled cheek with the back of a gentle hand. 'I know. I've had my little battles and skirmishes too. I've grown lazy – have gone native, as they say. I love this place. Not just Puerto Rico but my cottage, this old point up here where we're standing, the days of sunshine and the wonderful nights. The thought of going back chills me.'

'You wouldn't have to.'

'Oh yes I would. You're not exactly a beachcomber's wife-type, love.'

'Well, not to New England, anyway.'

He laughed. 'Are you proposing to me?'

She matched his mood with a little smile. 'I guess I am at that. Well?'

'I accept. But you have no idea what an idealistic dreamer you're getting embroiled with.'

'My uncle liked you, and he knows men.'

He reached, drew her closer, tipped up her face but didn't kiss her. For a moment they stood motionless looking at one another. Then he said, 'You have two weeks yet. Think it over very carefully. You see, I don't like New England. Oh, I like *visiting* there. I like visiting Columbus, Ohio, where I was born, and New York where I worked up with the oil company, but *this* is my world now.'

'I'll think about it,' she agreed. 'Now kiss me.'

He did, and she melted against him feeling every last shred of resistance crumbling. Afterwards he took her over to the Three Sisters and they stood there a bit before he softly said she had better go back or her uncle would begin worrying and all her guests would begin talking, which was even worse in a place like Puerto Rico.

She left him leaning against the cannons, waved and bumped down off the point to the dark, narrow road that would take her safely homeward.

She had heard a dozen different explanations of love and not one of them fitted. But she'd never before known a widower, a man who had given his heart and soul to another woman, and neither had she ever known a man who seemed so detached from the competitive, aggressive world of men like Frank McFall, and even her own father and uncle, who were also keen, predatory men, each in a different way but still predatory.

But perhaps most bizarre of all – as she'd told him – falling in love had never been farther from her conscious thoughts than when she'd arrived in Puerto Rico. Still, it had happened. She thought it may even have happened without her being quite aware it was happening; that first time she'd met him – sweaty, rumpled, but with that wonderful smile and those gentle, honest eyes – she'd felt *some* response.

She saw the lights up ahead and was relieved, it meant the guests were still there. It didn't occur to her that it was actually very late; too late, really, for people to still be partying.

She was simply too pleased to discover that her uncle wouldn't reproach her for being gone so long.

But when she drove round back and switched off the Land Rover she got the most peculiar sensation. It was as though everyone was in there *waiting* for her. She climbed down, arranged her dress and was starting forward when a soft voice called from deep shadows alongside the stable.

'*Señorita!*'

It was old Gregorio, and that surprised her. It was very late. He'd have no business being up and stirring at such an hour, unless one of the horses was ailing. She hesitated, then turned and, holding her skirt raised a little, ran over where the wizened old man stood.

'What is it, Gregorio; is a horse ill?'

He ignored the question. '*Señorita,* a bad thing happened while you were gone. You must be very brave, and you must also be very careful from now on.'

'What are you talking about?'

'*Señorita, el patron* died tonight.'

She stood in stupefied silence staring into the pinched-down, streaked and lined old leathery face. He nodded, correctly assessing her mood.

'While you were away. I don't know how it

happened, but I came here to await you. Please be careful what you say and do, *Señorita*.'

'Why? I don't understand.'

'Well, go now, and be in command of yourself. And if you need an old man, Gregorio is always close at hand. *Deo volante, Señorita*. Go with God.'

Gregorio turned on silent sandalled feet and disappeared around the side of the stable leaving Dolores still too stunned to move.

Others had seen the headlamps of the returning Land Rover. She heard them coming across the rear patio. She made out the pale, round face of Fred Gore first, then the ape-like silhouette of Frank McFall. Behind the burly man came Father Cordoba and others, a blurred mingling of movement in the latent starshine, for now the moon was far down and failing.

She heard their voices, felt their stares, sensed their gravity, and slowly poise returned. She sought the lovely face of

Rosaria Aldama but it was not present. She turned when gruff, massive Frank McFall took her arm and started her towards the house growling a little at the others to be quiet, to permit her to recover from the shock of what they'd all been mentioning.

She didn't resist, but with the resurgence of her old vitality she wished McFall were Whitney Jackson. She waited until they were clear of the others then said, 'What happened, Mister McFall?'

He was blunt, which was entirely in character for him. 'I don't know. Your uncle went into his study. We heard the shot. I reached the door first and looked in. He was lying on the carpet in front of his desk.'

'Shot?' she murmured, halting a yard from the patio and looking puzzled.

'In the head,' said McFall. 'Come along, I'll get you a drink. Fred called the local police-constable, but that's a waste of time. We'll have to get some of the qualified people from San Juan.' He used a little force getting her into the house, which still smelt of good food and liquor and fragrant tobacco-smoke.

The others came trooping in, funereal and silent. McFall called for a drink and that was when Dolores saw Rosaria. She was sitting loose and impassive upon the opposite side of the room looking totally unaware of everything that was happening around her. It struck Dolores that Rosaria suddenly had aged, but of course that could have been her own distraught imagination. Or it could have been the lighting, which someone had turned up pitilessly.

The drink came, Dolores downed it and nearly choked, then there was the sound of an ancient car coming in from the main gate and most of the remaining guests moved towards the door.

McFall, hovering nearby, leaned and said softly, 'Dolores, the police are here. Now remember – you are the lady of Estate Sao Paolo now. If you wish, you need tell them nothing at all. Not a word. But first thing in the morning you must contact your uncle's attorneys in San Juan to come up here and advise you.'

She raised her face. 'I don't understand what you mean, Mister McFall?'

Someone else might have been more reticent, less inclined to blurt out the thought that had to be in the other minds as well as in his own. Not Frank McFall.

'Dolores, everyone excepting you and the elder Gores were right here in the house when your uncle was killed.'

That was the shock that nearly paralysed her; he hadn't accused her of murder but he'd plainly and forthrightly stated what was a fact: she was most certainly a likely suspect.

Rosaria turned slightly and gazed directly at Dolores. Her golden eyes were as dull as old rust and her lovely, soft and sensuous mouth fell at the outer edges. She said nothing. She didn't even move when in the entry hall fresh masculine voices in rough Spanish were audible over the soft murmur of all the other voices. Then she turned her face away and resumed her impassive gazing out of a window beyond which the night was now dark and unfriendly.

Dolores had a feeling that Rosaria somehow was blaming *her* for what had happened. She wanted to say something, to protest. She even felt like crying but she controlled that impulse. As Frank McFall had said, she was now very much under study; she would be the lady of the Estate Sao Paolo. She couldn't cry. Not yet anyway. She rose as the guests came crowding back into the room surrounding two swarthy, none-too-neat *mestizo* constables whose unmistakable bloodlines were well rooted in the Afric ethos.

Chapter Eleven

SHOCK – AND REACTION

These negroid policemen were familiar with the routines of their job but beyond that they were hampered by the mentality of most blacks. One of them, perhaps feeling uncomfortable inside the house, said he would go and look round the yard and grounds. He didn't even wait to enter the study with his companion, a *café au lait* constable named Beadle, to view the corpse.

Constable Beadle seemed relieved to find Father Cordoba on hand. When he spoke he usually directed his questions and comments to the priest. Beadle also showed deference, but when he viewed Dolores Harper he seemed to have suspicions. He asked everyone to sit down in the large living-room and give him an outline of their movements for the entire night. Only when Dolores's turn arrived did Constable Beadle's coarse features and muddy complexion seem to lose all animation as he stolidly and stonily listened.

When Dolores said she'd driven Whitney Jackson to the promontory, Beadle, who had spent all his forty years in the Feliciano countryside, said, 'How long were you gone, Miss?'

Dolores felt the eyes of the others steadily staring. She knew it was not going to sound well, but she told the truth anyway. 'Perhaps an hour and a half, perhaps two hours.'

'Only to the promontory and back, Miss?'

Dolores blushed in spite of herself. 'Yes. But Mister Jackson and I stood for a short while talking, and admiring the night.'

Frank McFall, direct and brusque, said, 'Constable, there's a dead man in the study. These folks aren't going anywhere, so why don't you go see what you can make out of things in there, then complete your questioning?'

Constable Beadle seemed annoyed by McFall's attitude, but instead of answering back he looked at Father Cordoba, who very gently raised and lowered his shoulders. Beadle went back to his questioning.

'Miss Harper, was Mister Jackson out of your sight any of the time you were at the *barranca?*'

'No.'

'And you were not out of his sight?'

'No. Constable, I'm bewildered by whatever is behind this question.'

'Simple,' said the mulatto. 'You can give him an alibi, he can give you one. So if I find that either of you killed Mister Fitzgerald, then I will have to find a way around those alibis.'

Dolores stared at the constable. He shot Father Cordoba a glance then said no one was to leave the room until he returned from the study. After his departure Father Cordoba and Frank McFall looked at one another. McFall showed an expression of distaste.

'Is that the only constable, Father?'

'No, Mister McFall, there is the other one who went outside, but he only helps Constable Beadle because he is unable to hold any other job.' Father Cordoba smiled.

McFall saw no humour. He said, 'I'll personally call San Juan tomorrow and have skilled detectives sent up here.'

For a while there was silence. Outside, the sky was brightening very slightly off where the sea met eternity. A Caribbean sunrise would explode out of the east shortly, a fresh humid day would arrive – and Howard Fitzgerald would not be there to see it.

For Dolores, the last numbness departed, eventually. She could accept that which she could neither change, nor quite understand. Her uncle was the last person she ever would have imagined might kill himself or be killed.

Of course she had only been at Estate Sao Paolo two weeks, and had no idea what undercurrents might be silently running, but she knew her uncle, and it seemed impossible that he could have an enemy sufficiently motivated for murder.

She sought Rosaria with her eyes but the older woman remained stonily silent. She'd only broken her silence once since Dolores had returned. That was to tell the constable she had been dancing with Mister Fitzgerald only moments before he'd gone to his study. The constable had asked why he had gone in there and Rosaria had looked away without answering, beyond saying, 'You would have to ask him.'

None of the others had even known this much. They had been dancing, eating at the buffet, talking, or sitting somewhere with smokes, drinks, relaxed and satiated. With only one exception they had all said their last glimpse of their host had been while he was dancing with Rosaria Aldama. That exception was of course Dolores; she'd last seen her uncle hours earlier when she'd told him she was going to drive Whitney home;

he had been standing near a little rosewood tear-drop table near the doorway between the living-room and the back of the house, where there was a little soft-lighted hallway.

Constable Beadle returned, his muddy eyes baffled, his attitude somewhat altered as he entered the living-room. Frank McFall rose, truculent, defiant. 'I'm going home,' he announced. Constable Beadle did not contest this attitude, he simply nodded. He knew them all anyway, had their statements, and evidently Constable Beadle had reached the end of his personal resources.

They all left, and only one of them failed to come by and commiserate with Dolores. Rosaria went out into the soft chill of new dawn and stood quietly on the patio for a while, until all the others had driven off, then she turned when Dolores came to the doorway and said, 'I don't know why it should happen. I don't understand, do you?'

Dolores shook her head and Rosaria, acting as though she had actually expected a reasonable answer, turned finally and departed. Her car was the last vehicle to leave the grounds. She seemed the only one of them who had not been able to recover from shock.

Inside, the servants were being interrogated in the kitchen by Constable Beadle. Dolores went out there to listen.

But there was nothing. In fact, the servants knew even less than the guests had known, which was perhaps understandable; they had been busy with the food, the details of the party, had in fact paid small heed to their employer whom they took for granted, and had been engrossed with the other people.

Dolores went to her own quarters to bathe and change. The party-dress she laid aside in favour of more functional, sober daytime wear, seemed very much out of place now. When she returned to the living-room one of the servants brought her coffee and showed a sympathetic face. She asked if Constable Beadle were still around. He was not, the servant said. He had gone back to

Feliciano to make arrangements for the body of *el patron* to be taken away.

Dolores nodded and said, 'Find Gregorio and send him to me on the rear patio.'

She took her coffee out there to wait. After a time the old man came, hat in hand, peering at her out of slitted eyes.

'*Señorita?*' he said.

'Gregorio, when the constable was here talking to all the servants in the kitchen, why weren't you there?'

'*Señorita,* he did not call for me. Moreover, I was busy in the stable and–'

'Gregorio!'

'*Si, Señorita?*'

'You were called. *All* the staff was called. I want your reason for not coming.'

'*Señorita,*' said Gregorio, whining. 'I am an old man and I knew nothing anyway. There was no need for anyone to even consider old Gregorio.'

Dolores was not going to get a direct answer, that was more obvious each time she tried for one, so she tried a different approach. 'How did it happen you were awake, dressed and waiting last night when I got home?'

'I heard the gunshot, *Señorita*. It awakened me very much.'

'I see. But otherwise you slept soundly?'

'*Si Señorita.*'

'With all the loud talking, the loud music, the noise of all those people celebrating, you slept straight through without difficulty – but with the pop of one little gun you were instantly awake. Gregorio, you are a very great disappointment to me. I thought you were my friend, my good friend.'

The old face twitched. 'I *am* your good friend,' said Gregorio swiftly, '*Señorita*, I think I am even a better friend to you than the priest. I cannot help what you think, but I waited in the shadows last night so as to be able to warn you. And furthermore, I have gone even beyond that to prove I am your friend.'

'What do you mean?'

'I only just got back from below the old

fort, *Señorita,* so if you must know why I could not be questioned by Jorge Beadle – who is a fool anyway, I've known him all his life – now you know.'

'You went – for *Señor* Jackson?'

'*Si.* First, last night, I had to warn you to be very careful what you said. Secondly, I had to see that you had a man – *muy macho* – to look after you.'

'He is coming?'

'Yes, *Señorita.* I think he will arrive very shortly. He was only a little distance behind me and I've been back a little while.'

'But Gregorio, why didn't you just simply tell me this in the first place?'

The old man seemed a little irritated, as well he had every right to be; Dolores had handled him roughly. He said, '*Señorita;* I saw *el patron* through the window. When a person has been killed by an assassin, I have lived long enough to know that a prudent man becomes very unobtrusive, for otherwise, with the assassin still loose with his gun, an imprudent person can also become a victim. *Señorita*, the killer of your uncle can only die once for murder, no matter how many other people he also murders. So you must understand – I am being careful even though I am also being your good friend. But you act as though I am the assassin myself, and maybe it would be better if I went back to my little house in Feliciano and stopped working on the plantation.'

She *had* been suspicious of him, and if in afterthought her reasons did not seem too good, at least in her present emotional state they were perhaps understandable. She said, 'I'm sorry, Gregorio. Will you forgive me?'

'*Seguro, Señorita*. What is there to forgive? Now, I should get back to the stables. There is much to do.'

She let him go, finished her coffee, put the cup and saucer aside and no longer felt so lonely. She had two friends, an old mahogany-coloured, black and beady-eyed Cuban expatriate, and a handsome much younger Stateside expatriate.

One of the servants came to say the ambulance was coming through the front gate. She turned to enter the house, then turned back as someone spoke her name from a short distance off.

Whitney, breathing hard as though from the several-mile trot, was approaching. She was tremendously relieved. She did not want to have to enter the study and supervise what had to be done in there. As he came up she went into his arms. He patted her back a moment then released her.

She told him everything that had happened up to this moment, everything she knew, which was practically nothing, then she also explained about the ambulance outside, begging him to go with the men to the study and see that her uncle was properly taken away.

He left her. She heard the ambulance-men speak in subdued, rapid Spanish, heard Whitney fire back at them in the same tongue, then she heard all of them move away, deeper into the house. And that was when it finally hit her.

She wept. When it proved impossible to stop, she ran to her bedroom and fell across the un-slept-in bed and let the tears come. She had felt tender affection for her uncle. Some of the things he'd told her, usually with a joking twinkle in his eyes, like the time he'd said she would be mistress of Estate Sao Paolo when he died, came back now and troubled her.

She also remembered the laughter they'd shared, the discussion of his plans for the plantation, and she remembered his kindness, his warmth, his grey and distinguished good looks.

Prior to arriving in Puerto Rico she had known him only vaguely; he had visited Massachusetts twice, and both times she had been a gangling child. His letters, though, were what had drawn her to him. They were vivid, humorous, thoroughly delightful letters.

Her father, who actually was only her uncle's half-brother – they'd had the same mother and different fathers – had once said each generation had a few men like Howard Fitzgerald, but only a few. As she drifted off into an exhausted slumber, worn out from weeping, from sleeplessness, from shock, she agreed: each generation had only a few men like Howard Fitzgerald.

Chapter Twelve

A PUZZLE

Constable Beadle returned shortly after midday to ask if he could search the study. Evidently he had made a closer examination of the body down at the village, or possibly someone more shrewd than he, had done this, but in either case he was given the run of the house by Whitney, who explained that *el patron's* niece was sleeping, completely exhausted.

Beadle went to the study doorway and stood a long while just looking around. He eventually entered and began a systematic search. He may have lacked imagination, perception, intuition, but he certainly was dogged. By the time Dolores rose, bathed her face and went out into the living-room where Whitney was waiting for Constable Beadle to finish, Beadle was still not finished and it was mid-afternoon.

Whitney asked how she felt. She smiled ruefully. She felt rested, she said, but she also felt dull, heavy in mind and body, as though the long rest had drugged her. She wanted to know what the constable sought. Whitney could only say that Beadle had been very reticent when he'd returned to the house. But nonetheless Whitney had some idea.

'A weapon, I suppose. We looked around in there when they came to take your uncle away. There was no weapon; at least we didn't find one at that time.'

She said, wistfully, 'I wish we'd stayed, last night, Whitney.'

Wishes, generally, being useless little things he only nodded, then said, 'I've been walking around all day trying to imagine a motive.'

'And...?'

'I can't imagine one for the life of me,

Dolores. Possibly you can help.'

'But I know nothing of his private life. Except that he didn't seem to have one, outside of the estate, which was his love. Almost his obsession.'

'Then perhaps it was someone here, among the servants.'

She couldn't agree. 'But why? He has done more for them than their own government has done. You should have seen the tears in the kitchen this morning when the constable was questioning them.'

He said, 'McFall? Fred Gore? Rosaria?'

'It couldn't be – could it?'

'That's what I'm trying to fathom. If we'd been here perhaps we would know who was absent from the room when he was shot.'

'No one,' she said. 'Ask Constable Beadle. Last night – excuse me, this morning – he went over every story. They were verifiable among the guests, so unless someone lied to shelter someone else, it couldn't have been the guests.'

Whitney said, 'Constable Beadle interrogated me too. I would say he suspects either you or me, or perhaps that both of us together in a dark conspiracy, had something to do with it.'

'That's ridiculous, Whitney. We were miles away.'

'Of course. But he isn't prepared to accept that wholeheartedly, and actually I don't blame him.' Whitney looked up. Constable Beadle was standing in the doorway, evidently listening. He showed no embarrassment as he came forward, seated himself and looked glumly from one of them to the other.

'I don't know how it was done,' he said, speaking very slowly and ponderously, 'unless the murderer simply opened the study door, with his back to the hallway, fired, then quickly closed the door and hastened back to join the guests, or the servants.' He looked at Whitney. 'There is no weapon. There was no weapon last night. The windows are closed.' Beadle shook his head, thoroughly baffled. 'The others, even the servants, were all within sight of each other.' Beadle's muddy eyes were gloomy. 'Do you see?'

Dolores saw. 'In other words, Constable, you think Mister Jackson and I are involved.'

Beadle's gloomy stare lingered on her. 'Can you tell me what else I must believe?'

She couldn't. A chilling thought occurred. 'Are you saying we are to be arrested?'

Constable Beadle doubtless had some such idea in mind, but he was not investigating some drunken knifing among the villagers; this dilemma required extremely delicate handling. A constable's pay was not much, but then ordinarily the work was not difficult either, and in a place such as Feliciano unless a man chose to work in the fields on the plantations, his means of existence were very limited. Constable Beadle, in other words, was actually more concerned with his future welfare than with this accursed murder. And he shrank from the prospect of arresting the *patron's* niece, for if events turned out differently, somehow, from how they now looked, he could not only lose his job, he could be everlastingly disgraced. Neither notion had any appeal for him at all.

He resolved his situation weakly. 'There will be detectives here sometime tomorrow. They know more about these things than I do. I telephoned to San Juan this morning. What I ask is that neither of you go away; that you stay here on the estate.'

Beadle rose. He had said what he'd had to say and now he was anxious to leave. Dolores did not move. She nodded in response to Beadle's grave nod, and watched as Whitney escorted the constable out through the entrance hall. Then she rose, went to a window and gazed out where men were working in the nearest part of the citrus grove.

Everything seemed the same. It could have been a terrible nightmare, and her uncle could be out there somewhere with Hernan'

Godoy, supervising the work, which is the way he had spent his days. She turned when Whitney strode back into the cool large room. The look in his eyes made her face reality. It was *not* the same. Nothing would ever be the same again.

Whitney said, 'I think you should call your uncle's solicitors in San Juan – or someone, anyway, who can come out here and advise you.'

She nodded. 'I'll call my father. He'll fly down. He's one of the best attorneys in Massachusetts. He'll know what to do.' She returned to the sofa she'd vacated sat and said, 'I don't see how it could have happened if everyone can be accounted for.'

He waved that aside almost brusquely. 'Obviously everyone *can't* be accounted for, Dolores. Your uncle didn't commit suicide or the weapon would be there. Beadle has overlooked someone or some*thing*. The detectives from San Juan will work this out.'

It sounded so reasonable the way he said it that Dolores nodded. A telephone rang and a servant came to say she was wanted. It was Frank McFall; he wanted to know whether she'd like him to have his own attorney call and see her. She thanked him but declined, saying she'd ask her father to come at once. McFall then said, 'I've been wandering around the house since I got home trying to make sense out of it, and I can't for the life of me. I tell you, I was right there at the door. I was the first one into the study, Dolores, the smell of gunpowder was the only thing I encountered, except for your uncle – where he was lying. I can't see how anyone could have got in there, past me, and yet there wasn't a soul in the room ten seconds later.'

She was sympathetic and rang off as soon as she decently could. Back in the living-room again, she related what McFall had said. Whitney seemed preoccupied but he listened. After a bit he made a quiet suggestion.

'Rosaria was dancing with him. The way I got it from Constable Beadle he left her to go into the study.'

Dolores agreed; that was also how she remembered things.

'Why?' asked Whitney, gazing intently across the intervening distance. 'Why did he suddenly leave her and go into the study?'

'I have no idea. Perhaps he remembered something he had to do.'

'Shoot himself, or meet someone who would kill him? It doesn't make sense.'

'I have no idea, Whitney.'

'But we've got to know why he left her and went in there. He would have said something, wouldn't he? Perhaps a little excuse for leaving her.'

Dolores, thinking back to the stupefied condition of Rosaria Aldama, could only say what she'd heard Rosaria tell the constable. 'She said they'd been dancing. That Uncle Howard told her he'd be back in a moment, and went into the study.'

'Is that all she said?'

Dolores recalled nothing more, although admittedly she too had been in shock at the time of the interrogations. 'I think so. She acted drugged or too dumbstruck to react. She said Uncle Howard would be the one for Constable Beadle to ask, and of course he was dead so that didn't make sense. But at the time she was not herself. Later, on the front patio, she said to me she didn't understand why it should happen. She seemed to be moving through a dream. Even her actions, when she went out to her car, were very unlike her. She walked differently – more slowly, more like a sleep-walker would have moved. It was uncanny, but at the moment I could feel the same mood, or at least I thought I could.'

'I want to talk to her,' exclaimed Whitney. 'It's between Rosaria and the constable. But I don't think he's got anything. Or if he has, I don't think he realizes it.'

'What could he have, Whitney?'

He made an exasperated gesture. 'I don't know, obviously, Dolores, because if I *did* know we'd be that much closer to knowing what happened between the time your uncle left Rosaria and the time he was killed. A matter of a few minutes at the most.'

She considered. Her own condition was equal to the drive to Rosaria's estate, was equal to a discussion of what had happened. But, remembering Rosaria's condition after the tragedy and up until the older woman had left, Dolores was less certain Rosaria would be equal to going through another interrogation. Particularly the kind Whitney obviously had in mind – a tough, realistic one with no punches withheld.

But Dolores was tactful. 'Constable Beadle doesn't want us to leave the house.'

He brushed that aside with the same quick gesture of impatience he'd shown before, and she couldn't really condemn his reason. 'Dolores, the way things stand right at this moment it is you and I who are in deep trouble. Beadle won't arrest us. At least he won't arrest *you*. But I'm not so sure the detectives from San Juan will be so careful of stepping on toes. If we don't come up with something in our own defence, we could very well end up in jail in San Juan accused of murder. *Then* how could we help ourselves?'

She procrastinated a bit longer although she was inclined to support him. She said, 'Let me call my father first, Whitney. Then, if you wish, we'll drive over to the Aldama place.'

She left the room, went to her own quarters and sat down. She had no idea what luck she'd have reaching her father, either at home or at his office. She placed the call, was told it would take a few moments to make the connections providing all the trunks were not busy, and sat there gazing disconsolately at the telephone.

Whitney *was* right, of course. Whether he and she could turn up anything or not, the most logical place to begin trying was with the last person to whom her uncle had spoken moments before he'd died.

It might not be a very rewarding trip so soon after the tragedy, for as she remembered, Rosaria had seemed quite lost, totally unable to grasp reality, but if not today, then perhaps tomorrow. Sooner or later Rosaria would surely overcome the shock and return to rationality.

The telephone rang. It was her father; he'd been at his office, although it was very late in the day. She told him in a quiet, controlled voice what had happened. He did not interrupt. Evidently the shock had stunned him too.

She related everything that had occurred up to the time she was talking to him, being careful to enunciate clearly so there would be no misunderstanding. Their connection was excellent though. When he finally found his voice and spoke, it was almost as though he were no further away than the next town. He wanted to know who was suspected. She told him. 'Whitney Jackson and I.'

That stunned him into another moment of silence. Then he said, 'All right, Dee. I'll take the first flight out. Where do I land?'

'San Juan, the capital of Puerto Rico. I'll see that someone is there to pick you up. I'm sorry I have to break in on you like this.'

'Sorry,' he snorted. 'Just remember, child, say nothing, do nothing, until I reach you. The same goes for your friend Mister Jackson. Incidentally, do you know who Howard's lawyers were down there?'

'No.'

'All right. Forget it; I'll dig them up before I leave here. Sweetheart? Take care now, and don't worry. I'll see you soon.'

After she rang off she had to bite her lip to hold back a fresh rush of tears. She went to stand a moment by her bedroom window until the mood passed, then she returned to the living-room where Whitney was waiting.

Chapter Thirteen

A RIDDLE – A CLUE

They took the same Land Rover they had used the night before. Whitney added fuel from a storage tank that stood upon a steel platform beneath a huge, shady tree.

Dolores thought she saw Gregorio watching from the shadows of the stables but was not sure. It didn't really matter, although she had some unpleasant inkling that Constable Beadle might have left his none-too-bright assistant to spy on the house, making certain she did not leave.

If that were the case, Beadle's helper remained out of sight, because they drove down to the roadway and turned left heading for the countryside nearer Feliciano, without any kind of interruption. Of course, on an island like Puerto Rico, it was not always necessary to keep a close watch on people. The only three ways to leave the island were by ship, by air, or by little private boat, and the police had over the years perfected a very efficient method of controlling each of these avenues. Otherwise, running into the jungle to lose oneself, was nearly impossible, not to mention highly unpleasant for a man, but just about unheard of for women.

Dolores had never been to the Aldama plantation so Whitney drove. He was familiar with all the roads, fortunately, for there were forks, casual trails, broad avenues, crooked ruts, taking off from the main thoroughfare almost every mile or so. He did not deviate until, from atop a low brushy hill, they could look down upon the sleepy village of Feliciano, then he made a dry comment about not wishing to disturb Constable Beadle's siesta, and hooked the Land Rover hard to the right and went bounding and slithering over a back-road where little pools of water indicated one of the island's frequent, localized showers had fallen not more than a few hours before, probably during the night.

When they broke out of the gloomy, steamy jungle and encountered a wide savanna encircled by a tight wire fence, he told her they were paralleling the Aldama estate. The trees here were much older than the trees on her uncle's estate, and where the jungle had been pushed back there was some indication that oil had been sprayed along the borders to prevent indigenous growth from reclaiming the land.

They were, he said, coming to the Aldama place by a back route, one that ordinarily would be used only by workmen coming up from the village. The proper entrance was through Feliciano, then up a broad roadway maintained by the Aldamas for hundreds of years, and past a wrought-iron gate of elaborate design.

They eventually passed a less impressive entrance – hanging open – and pressed along towards the formal entrance. They were safe from the eyes of the curious villagers now, he told her, and swung through the formal entrance and began the half-mile drive over a gravelled roadway towards a two-storied, beautiful white colonial mansion set amid emerald lawns with huge trees keeping away most of the direct sunlight.

He told her what he knew of this place as they drove on up. This colonial mansion was the third or fourth villa to stand on the same site. One, the earliest, had been of stone, and during some half-forgotten civil disturbance it had been levelled by artillery. The second home had burnt, very mysteriously or so the old tale went, almost incinerating several Aldamas. The present mansion was either the third or fourth, local legend was unsure which, and it had been built by Rosaria's husband prior to his marriage and subsequent to a trip to the Virginian countryside of the United States. It was, Whitney thought, the most breathtaking reproduction of antebellum Southern plantation architecture in the entire West Indies.

When they halted and alighted, the great house seemed hushed and empty. There was no one in sight, not even a gardener although, as extensive as the grounds were, there had to be a considerable labour force somewhere around.

A dark-eyed maid opened the door for them, eyed them stoically and when Dolores said who she was and that she would like to see Rosaria, the little maid got upset. In sing-song Spanish she said that *el patrona* was not able to see anyone.

'Is she ill?' asked Dolores, and before the little maid could reply a stalwart houseman came silently to shoo her away and say his mistress, was, in fact, quite ill. That the doctor was coming from San Juan that very afternoon, and that while he regretted it abjectly, it would not be possible for either *Señorita* or *Señor* to see her.

Dolores studied the faintly negroid face of

the houseman. He was more Indian, more *Carib*, by far, than negro. He could have been forty or sixty. Also, he had the poise of a servant who knew precisely what to do in every circumstance. She said, 'Have the police been here this morning?'

The dark eyes didn't flicker at all. 'No, *Señorita.*'

He hadn't been the least surprised by her question. He therefore knew what had happened, and why his mistress was so distraught.

'Who telephoned for the doctor?' she asked.

The answer was firm and instantaneous. 'I did, *Señorita.* She arrived home this morning in a very bad condition. I am surprised she was able to drive here at all.'

'Did she know you?'

'No, *Señorita.* She did not seem to know any of us.'

Whitney plucked Dolores's arm. 'Come along.' He smiled at the houseman. 'Thank you – and I'm terribly sorry. If there is anything … but I suppose the physician will do everything.'

'Yes, *Señor*. When she is able I will tell her that you called.'

The door of the great house closed gently but firmly behind them. Silence as thick as endless layers of invisible gauze settled on all sides once more. Dolores shuddered and looked up. 'It's – unpleasant – here. Let's go back.'

Whitney was silent most of the way to the Estate Sao Paolo. Just before they made the turn into the drive he said, 'I had an odd feeling back there.'

Dolores vigorously nodded. 'I know. I had the same feeling.'

He eased on up to the house, halted, switched off the ignition and made no immediate move to climb out. He was scowling. 'She was in love with him.' He made something rather like a question of it. 'Otherwise why should she go completely to pieces; be in such shape a physician has to be brought all the way from San Juan?'

'The closest doctor, obviously.'

'Oh no. Father Cordoba is a physician.'

She stared in surprise. 'He is? I didn't know that.'

He reached, caught her arm and held her in the seat beside him. 'Did Father Cordoba look at your uncle last night?'

'I have no idea. I didn't hear anyone say that he had.'

'But wouldn't a physician do that, under the circumstances? Wouldn't he rush in and make certain your uncle was not still alive, perhaps thinking he might be able to save him?'

'I would think so, yes.'

'Hold on,' he said. 'This time we have to drive right through the village, and Constable Beadle is sure to see us. The monastery is on the far side of the village.'

'Whitney, can't we just telephone him? I don't think we should deliberately antagonize the constable.'

He paused as he leaned to punch the starter-button, gazed at her a moment, then

184

smiled at her expression of anxiety. 'All right. As you say. Let's go inside and use the telephone.'

The house was blessedly cool as compared to the rising heat, and humidity, that was building up outside. Dolores remembered that she had not eaten since the night before, and felt famished at once. She insisted they visit the kitchen before telephoning the priest down at Feliciano.

It was fortunate they went to the kitchen to see about something to eat instead of putting through the call to Alfonso Cordoba, because they were half through an impromptu meal when the priest came calling. He said he hadn't been at the monastery all morning, so if they'd tried to reach him there they'd have failed.

Dolores asked him if he were indeed a physician. Father Cordoba smiled and nodded. She then asked if he'd examined her uncle the night before. He shook his head negatively this time and when the two other people stared, he explained.

'I didn't have to. With the others I went to the study door in response to Mister McFall's outcry. There was no need to go any closer, Dolores.'

She said, 'You could be that certain?'

'Yes. Head-wounds usually prove fatal. Those that do not are miracles. The injury your uncle received was massive and inexorably fatal.'

'Then you made no examination, even after you knew he was dead?'

'No,' said Father Cordoba. 'For what purpose? Curiosity is in bad taste at a time like that. Besides, I wasn't curious – I was shocked, stunned, horrified to believe one of your uncle's guests could do such a horrible thing.'

Whitney studied the priest. 'Are you sure one of the guests *did* it, Father?'

Cordoba spread his palms wide. 'Who else? There was no one in the room, the curtains were drawn, the windows closed. A person could not see into the study from outside.

186

'You have some theory,' said Dolores. 'Will you tell us?'

Father Cordoba's expressive eyes showed pity and liking as they rested on her. 'No theory, really,' he said. 'I know the bullet struck him in the head, and since he had to be facing his killer when he was shot, I would say either the gunman was in the room with him – which just is not very probable – or else the killer was at the door, and when your uncle opened it, presumably because someone knocked, he was shot in the face.'

'McFall was standing by the door,' said Whitney. 'Did you know that, Father?'

Alfonso Cordoba was a shrewd, perceptive man. 'If you are asking – do I believe *Señor* McFall killed *el patron* – I would only say what I have already told everyone who asks: I don't know. I have no idea. The only things I am sure of at all is that *el patron* was dead before he fell to the floor of his study, and that everyone around me at the time, was just as stunned as I was.'

'Rosaria, Father?' said Dolores, and the priest's expression changed immediately.

'A terrible blow to her. She barely got home before she had a nervous collapse.'

'You treated her?' asked Whitney.

'No. Her *mayor domo* called as I was returning from the chapel this morning, before retiring but after I got back to the monastery from the party. He did not want me to come out, he wanted to know what should be done. I suggested he call her physician in the capital, and that he ask the women to put her to bed, keep the room dark, allow no visitors, and always have someone in the room with her.' Father Cordoba paused, looking mildly upset, then he said, 'I could have given her an injection so easily. It would have been no imposition at all, to drive up there and put her to sleep. Well, if they did not wish it, then that was their business, eh?'

'They – Father,' asked Dolores. 'Who are "they"?'

'Her *mayor domo*. The older retainers. She

inherited them along with the plantation, from her late husband – may he rest in peace. They have always been very protective.'

Whitney was nodding his head. Evidently, he knew this was so. Probably, he'd heard it from his fishermen-friends.

Dolores, who had not viewed the corpse, had not until this very moment been able to even discuss it, now was struck by something the others had said. 'Father, my uncle was lying face down, his back to the door, was he not?'

'Yes.'

'Well, is that the position you think he would be in if shot *facing* the door?'

Cordoba had apparently already considered that for he gently smiled as he answered. 'I can tell you that the blow was powerful, somewhat like being struck squarely in the face by a huge fist. It could have knocked your uncle ten feet back. It could have spun him either right or left. Or, it could have stretched him on his back instead of his stomach. Dolores, there is not very much to be learned from the position he was lying in, I'm afraid.'

It was true. Howard Fitzgerald had been struck too great a blow for that act to have done anything but kill him very violently without regard to details.

Father Cordoba, they said after he'd departed, had been no help. They were wrong but at this moment they had no idea how much of a help he had been. In fact, Father Cordoba himself had no idea he held a very vital clue as he went his quiet way.

Chapter Fourteen

FREDERICK GORE

Constable Beadle returned in the mid-afternoon looking stern. He had learned that *el patron*'s niece and her escort had visited the Aldama plantation after he'd instructed them not to leave Estate Sao Paolo.

It was only a minor infraction, Whitney claimed, and in any case no law could prevent people under strong suspicion from trying to clear themselves. Constable Beadle agreed that this sounded rational, and asked if they had turned up anything.

They had not, except that *el Señora* Aldama was suffering a nervous breakdown over the slaying. Beadle, who, like many 'progressives' in Puerto Rico, refused to employ the Spanish forms of address if they could possibly be avoided, merely shrugged over this information.

It was a known fact, he said solemnly, that Mrs Aldama was very friendly with Mister Fitzgerald. They had been seen together upon innumerable occasions over the past year or so, either hiking together or driving in either her car or his; moreover, she had presented him with several artefacts that had to do with island history, or the history of his estate, and it was known he was favourable towards her.

'She has every right to be in a state of collapse, I am afraid. I only hope she will not be removed to San Juan by her doctors because I must question her.'

'You have questioned the others?' asked Whitney.

Beadle nodded. 'Only one of them was not very co-operative. Young Gore. But his father told him to drive back to the village yesterday and answer my questions, so he did so.'

'And, Constable…?'

The muddy eyes were sardonic. 'Of course I couldn't tell you – either of you – because you are suspects and anyway, because the information would be restricted … Except that I have no information to protect. No one killed Mister Fitzgerald, it seems, or saw him killed, or has any idea that will help at all.'

'Have you spoken to Father Cordoba?'

'Yes. Several times in fact. What of it?'

Whitney shrugged. 'Nothing, I suppose, but it seems to me he was the only qualified person to see the corpse immediately after the slaying.'

'That is true,' assented Constable Beadle, 'but he recalls nothing that will help.'

Dolores, silently agreeing, had a suggestion to offer. 'Unless those detectives from San Juan have already departed, perhaps we should ask a qualified coroner to come to Feliciano.'

Beadle missed whatever innuendo was behind this and said, 'Your uncle will be sent to the capital today, as soon as the proper van arrives in Feliciano. As for your suggestion – I have never had any luck getting one of those people to visit a country village. I don't believe one of them would come even now.'

The conversation, beginning to drift and crumble from total lack of substance, was finally terminated with the departure of Constable Beadle, whose admonition was once again repeated.

'Do not leave the plantation!'

Dolores was puzzled by something. 'Do they always have their autopsies performed in San Juan? Wouldn't it be much cheaper and save a good deal of time if local physicians did those things?'

Whitney agreed that it probably would be more efficient, although he also professed to know nothing about such matters what-soever, and could therefore only advance one idea that occurred to him and seemed relevant. 'I doubt that ninety per cent of the rural villages have qualified people.'

They had sat through the visit with

Constable Beadle in the kitchen, but after he had left and they had finished luncheon, they went into the huge, lovely living-room where so short a while before there had been gaiety, dancing, music, and where now there was nothing but the echo of their voices and a feeling of melancholy.

Dolores sent one of the servants to bring Hernando Godoy to the house. She asked Godoy to take one of the local vehicles and pick up her father at the airport in San Juan.

Alice Gore called to express her deepest sympathy, and to also offer to do whatever she could. It was a generous offer, and a kindly one, but there really was nothing anyone could do until the police arrived, and there was even no guarantee *they* could do much.

A telegram arrived in mid-afternoon from Chester Morrison who was in New York, asking for instructions on how to act in the matter of a stock trade between companies Howard Fitzgerald had been concerned with.

Until she was reading the telegram it did not dawn on Dolores that she'd been guilty of a great oversight in not wiring Morrison concerning the tragedy. She did so at once, and upon returning to the living-room from her own quarters, where she'd telephoned the wire to New York, she heard voices out upon the rear patio and went to the door.

Whitney was out there talking quietly and earnestly to old Gregorio. They conversed in Spanish, which Dolores was not at all fluent in, like most Americans who had studied the language in school, but who also understood it passably well.

Gregorio turned and strolled away, in the direction of the stables, as Dolores reached the glass doors and went out on to the patio. Whitney looked at her.

'Did you send the telegram?' he asked.

She nodded. 'What did Gregorio want?'

He seemed to hesitate, then he said, 'When he came for me after the murder, I showed him a short-cut for getting here to your uncle's residence. It was past the old crypt. He was uneasy about passing it, but he did so. Just now he came to ask if I thought that might be the grave of Angelina Montoya. I told him that it was not; that I was quite positive it was the crypt of the historic holy man of this part of the island. He seemed to doubt that.'

She smiled. 'Because of the legend of the holy man rising to heaven?'

'He didn't say that was why he doubted, love, but he *did* say Rosaria Aldama would pay a fortune to anyone who found the grave of Angelina Montoya.'

'Did you tell him you knew where Angelina lay?'

'I told him nothing, and I don't think it would do any good in any case until Rosaria recovers from the shock of your uncle's death.'

She nodded, then said, 'Remember? There is something Gregorio may be able to help us with concerning Angelina.'

He remembered. He also said that Angelina and the holy man's crypt as well, had been forced into the background by this other, more current and serious matter. Then he said, looking thoughtful, that he had never before heard it said that Rosaria Aldama did not know where her grandmother was buried, or that she would pay a reward for this information.

Dolores, struggling between the slaying of her uncle and that earlier tragedy, shook her head. There were too many bewildering events. 'Rosaria,' she said, almost desperately, 'could help. I wonder if the doctors from San Juan have come yet, and whether they can't care for her here rather than after they take her away?'

One of the servants came silently to say there was a gentleman out at the front, Mister Fred Gore, to see Dolores. She thanked the servant and looked a little blankly at Whitney. Any other time he might have shown a whimsical grin; he had observed Frederick Gore's attentions towards Dolores at the party, but now he simply looked annoyed.

'I think I'll talk to Gregorio,' he said, making it rather obvious that he felt distaste for their latest caller.

Dolores went to receive the younger Gore. She was a little surprised, after what Constable Beadle had said about Gore's reluctance to return from the capital, to find him calling.

He explained that, almost breezily, as she led him into the living-room. 'Came back because of the constable, then stayed with my parents for a bit, and was still there when the detectives came calling. The day was spent anyway, after that, so I thought I'd drop by and see if there was anything I could help you with.'

Whether he'd meant for it to sound as it did, was anyone's guess. Dolores offered him a chair and would have sent for a drink but he declined. He was dressed in a lightweight gabardine suit, obviously expensive, and he managed to look cool in spite of the heat and humidity. She speculated that he had an air-conditioned car, and that otherwise, he spent as little time as possible outside air-conditioned buildings.

He studied her with a thoughtful, vague smirk. 'Anything new?' he asked.

She countered with a question of her own. 'Were those the detectives from San Juan who called on your parents?'

He nodded. 'Quite. They've been with Beadle, down in the village and now they're going about interrogating everyone who was at the party. I'm surprised they haven't got to you yet. But of course they will.'

She was antagonized by the way he looked at her, and by the way he said 'but of course they will', making it sound as though she were the prime suspect in her uncle's slaying.

Whatever she might have said in reply was headed off when he spoke again, saying, 'Terrible thing about Rosaria, of course.' He didn't sound as though he felt it were a terrible thing at all. 'But I suppose it was natural enough. After all, she was in love with your uncle – or hadn't you heard?'

'I knew she was fond of him. So was I. As near as I can determine, so was everyone who knew him.'

'Well, yes, I suppose. You're talking about his hired help of course. But that's not what I meant. I'm quite sure Rosaria wanted to marry him.'

That *did* irritate Dolores. 'How are you quite sure?' she demanded, emphasising the last two words, which were his, not her, words.

He shrugged, leaned back and slung one leg over the other one. 'Pretty common knowledge, Dolores-love. Not that there was anything wrong with it. He was single, so was she. They belonged to roughly the same generation.' His smirk lingered as he stared across at her. 'No one could have said she was after his wealth because she too is rich. It must have been love then, eh?'

She found herself detesting him. Not because of the things he said as much as the way he managed somehow to make them sound. Also, the way he boldly eyed her.

'Well, in any event the thing's done,' he went on, still breezy and bold. 'Now Estate Sao Paolo belongs to you.'

'Does it? How do you know that?'

His smirk broadened. 'Common knowledge, love. But even so, you're not going to be able to manage it alone. After all, the expenses will be ruinous, and the work very difficult for a woman. Granting that your uncle also left you his fortune, you're going to need some full-time help around here.'

She smiled very sweetly. 'Are you offering?'

He looked at her, perhaps trying to guess whether that sweet smile was genuinely sweet or whether it was a female trap. He said, 'If you want me, I'll come out here of course.'

She had to let the sudden anger that boiled up slowly boil away again before answering, but even in its aftermath she had that same urge she'd felt before when he was with her. She wanted to slap his smirking face. She said, 'I'm grateful. It's very kind of you to offer. But I have Godoy and old Gregorio.'

'You omitted one,' he said, rising. 'The beachcomber, or hippie, or whatever he is; the chap who lives in the stone shack down below the old fort.' He wasn't smiling now. 'Well, I'll be running along, love. You can always contact me through my parents.'

She saw him out then leaned upon the door struggling to control her wrath. He was utterly impossible. Arrogant, egotistical, snide; she blew out a big breath, then went towards the doorway leading to the rear patio.

She had to tell *someone* how much she loathed Frederick Gore and Whitney Jackson was the first one she thought of.

He wasn't on the patio so she headed for the stables. He and old Gregorio were sitting in tree-shade quietly talking in soft Spanish. Gregorio was fluent, if not very grammatical, in English, but he seemed almost at home in Spanish. Before she got round where they sat she heard Gregorio say in soft Spanish, 'My friend, when I was a young man there was much talk, but all I am sure of was that the *Señorita* was known never to have been seen again, and my *patron*, Don Francisco, once told me that it was very easy in the old days for the landed families to hide such things as murder. But he also told me since no one could prove that the poor *Señorita* was dead because there was no body, then there could be no proof of murder. Do you comprehend?'

Chapter Fifteen

THREE MYSTERIES

Whitney evolved a theory and they were sitting in the living-room of the *hacienda* when he explained it to her.

'We know Angelina was buried in haste; the grave tells us that much. But there were all those wrappings, and that meant she was buried by someone who cared. Otherwise, he'd simply have dug the hole and dumped her in it.'

Dolores was prepared to agree tentatively. Not that she was following his train of thought so much as she was pleased that he would use her as his sounding-board.

'Would a furious murderer wrap her so tenderly – and not remove the jewellery. I think not. It seems to me – and I think I have some basis for this – that Francisco Aldama did not bury her after shooting her. I am also convinced he didn't send some peons to do it, the obvious reason being that *peons* talk, and that could have got him hanged.'

'Who then?'

'The *Yanqui.* Her sailor-lover. Why else was she shrouded in the canvas sail of a boat?'

Dolores slowly nodded. And the jewellery, beyond cash-value, would mean nothing to a man stricken by grief, who was secretly burying his love. But there was something else that also occurred to her.

'The *detail* of the murder seems clear enough,' she said. '*Don* Francisco didn't actually find them in each other's arms. He found her at the trysting place, alone. Either before her lover arrived, or, more probably, after her lover had gone – after Francisco Aldama had witnessed their lovemaking. *Then he shot her.*'

Whitney looked intense as they fitted the

pieces of their century-old mystery together. 'And left her for the *Yanqui* to find – and bury. That would be the Spanish way; cruel but highly effective.'

He leaned back in his chair. For a moment they gazed at one another. They had solved something that had been an island mystery. Or at least they had come very close to solving it. Closer, in fact, than anyone else had come in over a hundred years, and they had done it without actually being very concerned. At least not at first, but now they were concerned. In fact, now they were *involved,* and if the game of *ancient* murder seemed somehow intertwined with *modern* murder, it was entirely understandable that they should feel the connection without saying they felt it, even between themselves, because in broad daylight and in an enlightened age, it seemed too preposterous.

The detectives from San Juan arrived about this time, scattering their thoughts of the oldtime slaying and forcing them to concentrate on the recent one. It was an easy transition, though, for bridging a century was not difficult when one's thoughts were wholly intent upon acts of fatal violence.

One of the detectives did precisely as Constable Beadle's assistant had also done; after bowing to Dolores and eyeing Whitney Jackson with circumspect irony, he went into the back of the house to interrogate the servants. The remaining detective, a polished, suave man named Roberto Gomez but who had very blue eyes and light skin, although his hair was jet-black and his nose had the faintly high-bridged, hooked look of oldtime Spaniards, proved his sophistication by being open and affable and acted more as a friend than an inquisitor; but of course that was the secret of his success as a detective too.

He asked to hear Dolores's version of what had occurred. He also wanted Whitney Jackson to tell all that he knew. Of course, since neither had been present, it did not take long to get this told. Then, Detective

Gomez wanted the details of that visit upon the promontory, explaining his reason simply.

'The element of time is important. If you, Miss Harper, were with Mister Jackson for two hours, then it either clears you entirely because you were too distant to have committed the crime, or else, or else it gave one or both of you ample time to get back here *and* commit it.'

Gomez shrugged, smiling at them the way a wolf might grin at cornered prey.

'I'm sorry. But wouldn't you prefer me being frank with you?'

Dolores had to smile. Detective Gomez was an unusual policeman. He was so candid, so sympathetic, that he drew people out in their desire to be helpful. She liked him.

Whitney seemed to also like him, for he said, 'Mister Gomez, there is a little chart hanging beneath the petrol tank where the mileage has to be written each time a vehicle is fuelled. I saw it when I loaded the

Land Rover up before we drove to the Aldama estate today. I think that may be your clue as to whether the car we used the night of the slaying returned to the *hacienda* after we left that night, or whether it did not.'

Gomez beamed. 'Very good, Mister Jackson. Excellent. I'll go look at that after a bit. And now, tell me, Miss Harper: who were your uncle's enemies?'

She couldn't help there and explained why. 'I've only been on the island two weeks. In that time I've never seen anything among the workers but respect and affection for my uncle. Otherwise, except for the party the night he was killed, I have met very few of his social friends.'

'But he may have said something; may have made some little remark.'

'I'm terribly sorry, Mister Gomez...'

The detective's blue eyes twinkled. 'That is all right. All I want is for you to tell me the truth. You don't have to stretch a point to please me.' He grinned at her. 'You would be surprised how hard the *peons* try to help; they tell me what they think I want to hear, and it sends me all over the island chasing rainbows.'

Whitney said, 'Mister Gomez, have you seen Rosaria Aldama?'

The detective's smile vanished; he turned a keen, questioning look upon Whitney. 'No. As I understand it she is unable to see anyone today.'

Dolores and Whitney raised their heads slightly. 'Today' held promise that her breakdown might not be as complete as they'd thought. Detective Gomez went on speaking.

'We have heard from every source she was in love with Mister Fitzgerald, and if that is so, why then her grief can be very understandable.'

When Gomez finished speaking he fastened his bright, probing gaze upon Dolores. He seemed to wish for her to volunteer either an affirmation or a denial of this rumoured affair between her dead uncle and Rosaria Aldama.

Dolores smiled again. This time because she was being drawn out by Gomez in a subtle way. He seemed to always manage to pull information out of people voluntarily. It amused her because she knew exactly what he was doing, whether he thought this was so or not.

She said, 'Mister Gomez, my uncle only mentioned Miss Aldama to me a few times in little offhand remarks. I'm sure he was fond of her. *How* fond I can't say.'

'And she?'

'I don't know. We've only been together twice. The last time was at the party. The other time was when he asked her to drop by one day and keep me from feeling lonely. She liked him, I could tell that, but she did not go out of her way to tell me how much, and of course I didn't ask.'

'Of course,' murmured Gomez, looking satisfied. 'Well, it is a mystery, all this.' He rose glancing around the handsome, large room. 'But I think it will fit a pattern.'

That intrigued Dolores as she also stood up. 'A pattern, Mister Gomez?'

His blue eyes were kindly and attentive when he replied. 'Murder follows patterns. Motivation varies, and the pattern varies with it. If one can discover some kind of valid motivation – hatred, envy, deceit, blackmail – it usually follows that the pattern will lead to someone.'

Whitney, rising, looked closely at Gomez, who had interrogated everyone, or at least *nearly* everyone who had been present at the party. He said, 'Some kind of pattern must be emerging, then. By now you must have some inkling.'

Gomez looked at Whitney. He was a shorter but thicker man. 'None at all,' he said. 'Isn't that strange?'

They all three paced slowly through to the entry hall, and there, when Dolores said she'd go tell his companion that Gomez was leaving, he bowed and thanked her, then, as she strode away his pleasant blue eyes followed her. He sighed and said, 'Mister

Jackson, you have a very interesting background.' The blue eyes slowly came back and rested on Whitney's face. 'You were in the employ of an American oil company in Cuba. You had a perfect cover, didn't you?'

They stood looking at one another, silent and unsmiling. Whitney said nothing. Gomez shrugged. From down the nearby corridor came the sound of a man and a woman hiking forward.

Finally, Whitney said, 'You're pretty thorough.'

Gomez nodded and looked up, lazily smiling. 'It pays. But you would know, wouldn't you? Central Intelligence Agency people are trained in thoroughness. Well, one request, please, Mister Jackson.'

'Yes, I know. Don't leave the area.'

Gomez grinned and offered a thick, hard hand. 'You see? We are both thorough. And we will meet again I'm sure.'

Dolores saw them shake hands as she and the other detective approached. She said nothing of it until the policemen were gone and she had led him back to the cool parlour.

'He is the most fascinating policeman I ever saw,' she laughed. 'I was expecting some great, rude hulk with suspicious eyes. He's positively fascinating. And he even shook hands with you when he left. That doesn't make it seem he views us as suspects.'

Whitney went to a window and said, with his back to her. 'I haven't been entirely frank with you, Dolores. The reason Gomez and I shook hands was because we understood something that made us a little alike.'

'Alike...?'

He turned. 'I wasn't just an oil-company manager in Cuba. I was an agent for the Central Intelligence Agency.'

She took that in her stride. 'Whitney, I never for a moment thought you would be *just* an employee, no matter whom you worked for.'

'I was a spy.'

She nodded. 'Good for you. I suppose we need a lot of them around the world nowadays.'

She took his arm and pulled him away from the window. 'I won't say I suspected that when you told of being pursued by that Cuban gunboat, or whatever it was, but I *did* wonder why a supposedly responsible American and his wife would leave Cuba in a small motor-launch in the middle of the night.'

'One jump ahead of the Secret Police,' he muttered, and let her lead him to the sofa where they both sat down.

She sighed. 'I'm not sure I'm capable of keeping ahead of all these mysteries, Whitney.'

He smiled at her. 'Two of them are rather along towards being solved, I think. Anyway, *my* mystery is a very minor one. I was not a special spy, just a working model. The special ones rarely get caught. They are professionals. I wasn't and somehow the Cubans caught on. I was tipped off and provided with a boat. You know what happened.'

'Was your wife also in the employ of the C.I.A.?'

He nodded without speaking.

The telephone rang somewhere in the rear of the house. A servant came.

It was Dolores's father; he had arrived in San Juan, had spent several hours there talking to the attorney who had served his half-brother, and was calling to say he had located Hernando Godoy and would very shortly now be leaving the city for Estate Sao Paolo. He wanted to be assured she was all right, that everything at the plantation was peaceful.

Dolores said, 'Dad, it couldn't be peaceful, but it's safe enough and quiet. Whitney and I'll have supper waiting when you come along. How was the flight down?'

'Terrible! We had to skirt around a typhoon. It was bumpy and I'm not accustomed to this heat. You could, if you really wished to humour an old man, have something tall, tinkly, and alcoholic, waiting at the door when I arrive.'

'Promise,' she laughed, rang off and went to tell Whitney. He was over standing by the shaded window looking off over the treetops towards the promontory, and turned slowly, unsmiling, when he spoke.

She could guess his troubled thoughts. It made her wonder one more time what widowhood did to a man's mind, and whether or not one woman could ever really take the place of another woman.

She decided, with a surge of combativeness, she would try as hard to make it work as she'd ever tried anything in her life.

Then he smiled that gentle, kindly smile of his, and she forgot everything except that he was there with her, and *had been* with her throughout all the pain and unpleasantness up to this time. She ran to him, threw both arms around his neck and gave him a bold, fierce kiss. Then she jumped back because his arms came up swiftly, reaching.

Chapter Sixteen

GUEST FROM NEW ENGLAND

Dolores's father was a lanky, rawboned individual who looked as though he'd be more at home upon the bow of an oldtime Yankee Clipper, spy-glass in hand, than standing in a courtroom. He did not resemble his dead half-brother except in a quite general way, but there was no mistaking the fact that he was accustomed to authority. It was also fairly evident that he did not like the situation he now found himself in, and after the preliminaries were done with and he had been pleasant with his daughter and Whitney Jackson, he got straight to the point.

'Howard's attorney in San Juan showed me a copy of his Will. Everything goes to you, Dolores – after taxes and other obligations are met and satisfied. That, my dear, is exactly what the police seem to attach the greatest significance to.' He lit a cigar and his eyes brightened for the first time. It had nothing to do with his thoughts, though. 'Wonderful cigars,' he said. 'Superb. I was afraid to ask in San Juan, and although I note the Puerto Rican address of the maker, I've smoked enough Cuban stogies in my time to think these came from Havana. Well, back to it, eh? All right; the law here isn't very different from the law back home. Howard's attorney assured me of this. But, not being licensed here, of course I can't represent you in court. I've taken care of that through Howard's man in San Juan.

'Now then, what's *got* to be resolved is who, exactly, killed Howard.' At the look on Dolores's face her father threw up a hand. 'I know – everyone wants that answer including the detectives from San Juan. But there is a big difference where you two are concerned. If the police don't find someone, they're going to bend circumstances to make it appear one or perhaps both of you, killed him. Not villainously, but the police will not accept a verdict of "killer or killers unknown" as long as they have a single decent suspect.'

'Us,' said Whitney, and the older man nodded. A servant came to refill their highball glasses. Whitney and Dolores declined but Dolores's father did not. He even smiled as he handed over the glass.

After the servant's departure he took up the matter of the murder; he wanted details and all they could give him were the identical facts everyone already concerned also knew. But even then, they could only repeat what they had heard, neither of them having been present when Howard Fitzgerald had died.

It wasn't enough, he said, and Whitney, at least, was not very surprised. 'McFall,' he said, 'was the first man into the study. Rosaria Aldama was the last person to whom Mister Fitzgerald spoke. You can see McFall, I'm quite sure. As for Rosaria, it may be some time. She had some kind of emotional collapse. But unless they will remember something neither of them mentioned earlier, then what we've told you is exactly what they will also tell you.'

Dolores's father jumped to his feet. He was an incisive, direct, energetic individual. 'Show me the study, will you please, Dee?'

She led the way and Whitney Jackson brought up the rear. The older man, highball grimly in hand, still had not rested from his flight, but it didn't seem to bother him very much.

The study was an elegantly masculine room where very little expense had been spared. Along the north wall bookshelves ran from floor to ceiling, with two breaks where windows were located. These were both closed and curtained. Whitney mentioned these facts because he saw the question coming.

'The windows were closed, locked, and

curtained, Mister Harper. Also, as you can see by looking behind the curtains, no one has dusted back there in a 'coon's age.'

Harper went and looked.

The south wall was also book-lined, but since it also formed a partition with the adjoining room there were no windows.

The east wall, on the front of the house, had not only a very large, plate-glass window permanently fixed into the wall, it was also flanked by two smaller windows which were always kept open. The circulating cool air from the patio where no sunshine could reach, kept the study pleasantly cool.

Dolores's father pounced on what had been obvious to everyone who had visited the study subsequent to the killing. He even went over there and pantomimed a stealthy killer approaching the window from out upon the patio, raising a gun and firing. Both Dolores and Whitney started shaking their heads even before her father had finished. Whitney faced the north wall.

'He was facing in this direction, I'm quite sure, when the bullet hit him squarely in the face.'

Harper said, 'But that's impossible. The widows over there were not open. Otherwise, someone would have to have been, not just inside the room with him, but less than ten feet distant.'

Whitney nodded. 'Exactly.' He turned, pointing. 'And that is the only door. So, after shooting your brother, Mister Harper, the murderer had to either step around his falling body, or step over it as it fell, get to the door, open it and get out unobserved – with Frank McFall already alerted by the gunshot, and coming forward. Not to mention several guests who were also close by, and who would have seen anyone dashing from the room. They all claimed they saw nothing like that at all.'

Harper screwed up his forehead. He walked over in front of the desk, faced north, then looked down where his half-brother had died. He scratched the tip of his nose a moment, brightened and said, 'Suicide!'

Dolores crushed that. 'There was no weapon. This room has been searched three or four times. The detectives from San Juan haven't gone over it, but I expect them tomorrow. Dad, *there is no explanation.*'

He snorted. 'Of course there's an explanation. For heaven's sake, Dee, there is an explanation for *everything.*'

She stood with Whitney, saying nothing and gazing at her father with an attitude that plainly challenged him to prove his words.

He moved over the room with great care, almost with an attitude of exaggerated concentration. Dolores and Whitney waited, willing to help any way they could. He did not call upon either of them, and eventually, returning to where they stood near the doorway, he dug out another of those golden cigars, lit it leisurely, savoured the bouquet, the taste, then swore.

'Damn it to hell, Dolores, don't just *stand*

there! Tell me what the police think, what *anyone* thinks about how he was shot. This is utterly preposterous. There is no such thing as a total mystery ... Whitney?'

Jackson smiled gently and shook his head. 'I have no idea how he was killed, sir.'

Dolores reached, patted her father's arm and took him back into the lighted sitting-room where servants had come during their absence to clean ashtrays, light lamps, freshen up the room a bit.

Outside, nightfall was at hand. The three of them went out to the front patio and sat where the first breezes of evening reached. It was very pleasant; not humid for a change.

Dolores peered at her father. There was a moon but under the roof of the overhang shadows were in dark layers. She said, 'Aren't you tired, wouldn't you like me to show you to your room?'

The answer was brusque. 'Of course I'm tired. Furthermore that damned airplane frightened me half to death. But I won't be able to sleep until I understand how Howard was murdered.'

'I think you will,' said Dolores softly. 'Otherwise you're likely to be awake an awfully long time, Dad.'

Harper asked the question that occurred to everyone sooner or later. 'What did the coroner say, or hasn't there been sufficient time yet to have a post mortem?'

'The body,' said Whitney, 'was to be sent to San Juan today. There evidently are no local facilities at Feliciano.'

Harper looked surprised, then irritated. 'There is a physician in Feliciano, is there not?'

'Yes, but–'

'Well for heaven's sake, what else can these people find to procrastinate about!'

'Dad,' said Dolores, trying to finish what she knew Whitney had tried to explain. 'The local physician is a priest–'

'What of it, child; a good many church-men are also physicians, even surgeons and psychiatrists.'

'He feels that to intervene would be to intrude.'

'Good Lord,' groaned Harper, and blew cigar smoke at the slow-passing old moon. Then he straightened up, squinted at his wrist and said, 'Does this good father reside at the old stone monastery I saw when I came through your village this evening? Good, well then, suppose we drive down there right now.'

Dolores was taken aback. 'Whatever for?'

'The man was here, at the party, wasn't he; and he saw Howard's body and is a trained medical observer. What more do you want, love?'

'Father, he doesn't know a thing. He already explained that to Whitney and me. He didn't enter the study nor examine Uncle Howard. There is no point in going down there right now and getting him out of bed.' Dolores rose, stiff and looking slightly annoyed with her parent. 'Come along now, I'll show you to your room.'

Whitney sat down after Dolores and her

father had disappeared inside the house. He grinned in the night; Mister Harper was an aggressive, energetic pragmatist. He knew there were simple facts and he wanted them delivered to him. Of course, Detective Roberto Gomez also wanted them.

The hell of it was – thus far at least and regardless of all the talk – the only actual fact in the entire mess was that Howard Fitzgerald was dead.

Dolores returned, smiled a trifle ruefully and said, 'You'll have to forgive him, Whitney. He has that brusque, Yankee way about him.'

'I like him,' said Whitney. 'If anyone ever finds out what really happened in that damned study, I'll wager he'll be the one.' Whitney rose slowly, stepped to the edge of the patio and stood peering up and out, over the star-washed splendour of another cool and benign Puerto Rican night. 'Take a drive with me,' he said, 'to the old fort.'

She got out of her chair, went over to him and put her fingers inside his hand, then leaned. 'All right. Nothing else can happen, can it?'

He smiled, slid an arm round her waist and led her down from the patio into the smoky moonlight where the soft breeze continued to reach them.

Out back where the Land Rovers were parked, already re-fuelled for the following day, with their mileage properly recorded and the other details of operation and maintenance cared for, they selected the vehicle they'd used earlier, for the drive to the Aldama plantation.

He drove this time, slowly and expertly. She hadn't changed after dining, and therefore was hardly dressed for rough-riding over the plantation, but when they arrived up at the promontory where there was no underbrush, where in fact there was no growth at all out upon the gritty surface of the headland, her dinner dress was no hindrance.

But it may have been, as Whitney smilingly told her, the most elegant attire of any woman who had visited the *castella* since the first watch was kept for pirates.

She smiled back, flattered, but also pleased because she was convinced that he meant what he said.

They stood near the cliff-face with nothing but that old crumbling stone wall between them and a perpendicular drop to death upon the jagged rocks below where seawater churned and boiled.

The night was still up here, as quiet as death itself. The little breeze that had been playing back around the villa, was absent from the promontory. So was all sound and movement.

The Three Sisters kept their eternal, vain vigil over a grid of sea where no privateers had sailed in centuries. Past and present merged and formed a matrix of per-manence.

He felt it and said, 'This damned situation...'

She touched him and lay her head upon his shoulder. She was confident. Perhaps it wasn't confidence at all, but rather faith in him rising from her love for him. In either case she wasn't thinking altogether of her uncle's murder.

'Don't worry love,' she whispered.

He turned with her and paced across where the little guns were. Below, past the flourishing bougainvillaea bush, was the barely discernible trail leading to his stone cottage. He considered it a moment then sighed. Everything down there where shadows lay dark, belonged not just to another phase of his life, it also seemed to belong to a past that was beyond recall.

Chapter Seventeen

THE MATTER OF AN AUTOPSY

Detective Gomez inadvertently walked into what must have been something of a shock to him, the following day when he visited the Estate Sao Paolo alone, and in an open-throated sports shirt – not the type of thing he'd wear in San Juan at all.

Dolores's father met him in the parlour and pounced without warning. 'Neither my daughter nor Mister Jackson will answer any questions, Mister Gomez, excepting those directed specifically to what they know of Mister Fitzgerald's slaying.'

Gomez said, 'But, Mister Harper, neither your daughter or Mister Jackson were in the house at that time, so they could tell me nothing.'

'That, my dear Mister Gomez, is precisely my point!'

Dolores and Whitney were in conference with Hernando Godoy. It was of course inevitable that the plantation could not operate itself, particularly since it was still in the stage of development. On the other hand, except for Hernan', neither Dolores nor Whitney Jackson had the faintest idea what the defunct owner had had in mind, nor even how he proposed to achieve the ends he was aiming for.

Godoy was helpful in another way as well. Dolores was a city-girl, Whitney too, was ill-fitted by background for the rural existence even though he persisted in adamantly refusing to give it up. It therefore fell to *el patron*'s overseer to not only carry the entire load but to also have enough patience left over to indoctrinate his pair of novices. He was equal to the undertaking, primarily because he was by nature a pleasant, some-what tolerant individual. He also happened to be a very progressive and seasoned plantation *mayor domo*. One was entitled to wonder if his late employer hadn't in fact chosen him as overseer for precisely these attributes.

By the time the conference on the back patio was finished, the one in the living-room had resolved into a skirmish. Detective Gomez had used his charm, his subtleties, his disarming candour, and each had in turn been beaten down by the inflexible granite of the New England ethos. By the time Dolores and Whitney Jackson entered the room, Gomez and Dolores's father were sitting, over coffee, quietly discussing the slaying of Howard Fitzgerald as though neither had tried the defences of the other. Gomez was saying that Rosaria Aldama had not been thought by her San Juan physician to need the lengthy and distant care others had felt might be the case. He was remaining at the plantation with her for a few days, however, to make certain that recovery was properly implemented.

Dolores was pleased to hear this. Whitney seemed equally as pleased, although one was entitled to wonder, from his expression, whether his pleasure derived from the same humanitarian sentiments.

Dolores's father drove straight to the point, asking when Detective Gomez would be able to see Rosaria. Gomez only shrugged. The physician said it might be the next day, if her condition continued to improve, but he would not definitely commit himself.

Their visit was abruptly interrupted by a telephone call for Detective Gomez from Constable Beadle down in the village. It appeared that the van which had been expected to arrive in Feliciano the day before to transport Howard Fitzgerald's remains to the pathologist in San Juan, had been involved in some kind of smash-up the evening before, and would not now be able to arrive for perhaps another two days, unless of course the officials back in San Juan would agree to despatch another van.

Gomez was not particularly disturbed. He told the others, then said he thought he would go down to Feliciano and have another little talk with the curate, Father Cordoba.

That statement galvanized Dolores's father, who sprang out of his chair. 'Inspector,' he said, addressing Gomez by a title which, although appropriate, was not used on the island. 'Inspector, what would it take to get this priest to perform an autopsy right here, this morning?'

Gomez frowned. He did not know. He had to confess that in the capital where these matters were handled in a traditional and routine manner, he had never before encountered any deviation from the norm.

Harper said, 'All right; under the law in most of the places I'm familiar with, the body is the property of the heirs, the family, those concerned for its welfare. That being the case I am perfectly agreeable to an autopsy in Feliciano by the only qualified physician.'

Gomez gazed unhappily upon Harper. 'I can telephone,' he murmured, and didn't finish the remark. 'Of course it is essential that an autopsy be held.'

'And you might explain to your superiors in San Juan that the delay here in the country, is causing jeopardy to your case.'

Gomez nodded again, still considering the older man unhappily. Patently, for all his experience, this case had no precedents in Detective Gomez's former cases. He turned to Dolores and she, anticipating him, led the way to the nearest telephone.

When Whitney was alone with Harper he said, 'I assume your insistence is based on the fact that this is an unexplored avenue.'

Harper shot back a prompt answer: 'Well, isn't it?'

Dolores returned and moments later Gomez also came back to the room. He was looking thoughtful but he nodded. 'You will have to sign some papers,' he said. 'Routine, permission for this village physician to perform the autopsy. My superior says our bureau must be absolved of any responsibility.'

Harper smiled. 'Let's get on down to the village.'

Whitney went after the Land Rover but when he pulled round front only Dolores was waiting there. Her father, she told him, had gone on ahead with Detective Gomez, in the latter's car.

As they were driving out of the yard Whitney looked down and smiled. 'Your father is a very direct person,' he said. 'I wouldn't wonder but that he turns up something at that.'

She was less positive, but then she was thinking of Father Cordoba's last words when they'd discussed the murder. He had not wished to intrude. It was very possible he would say the same thing about performing an autopsy.

Whitney scattered those thoughts with a disconnected statement about Rosaria. 'Three days I would guess, are enough for even the deepest grief to begin to abate.

Reaction sets in.' He did not say he was speaking from experience but Dolores got that impression.

They came down into the dusty plaza of Feliciano, saw people stop to frankly stare, then drove slowly past dirty urchins playing in the gutters, past hordes of gaudy-plumed little runty chickens busily and unconcernedly scratching in the centre of the road, and even saw a great sow lying in a shady mud puddle, only her back and ears and little beady eyes visible, as she too watched their careful passage.

Feliciano was, like just about every old Latin American village, dominated on its outskirts by a very impressive mud cathedral. Beyond this structure, gloomy and ancient, stood a freshly constructed school whose architecture was modern, which is to say it was square and functional and depressingly ugly. No love had gone into the fashioning of its walls, as had been the case with the church and with the older homes. It looked – and definitely was – built in haste so that a backward country might grapple mightily to catch up with the twentieth century. Whether this bright ideal could ever be realized was another thing altogether, but at least the effort was being made.

The monastery was behind the mud cathedral, and except for the devout brothers who lived in that tiled-roofed old cool structure whose walls, also of adobe, were four feet thick on all sides, it was fair to assume that the ancient cathedral, built no doubt in a day when it had been the focal point for a vast countryside, would not have been in such good condition.

The peasants, devout enough, were nonetheless more concerned with making a living than with spiritual matters which, in any case, would be looked after by the brothers of the monastery.

Father Cordoba met his visitors in a sun-splashed courtyard, dressed in the clothing of a *campesino* – a peasant farmer. It took Dolores's father a moment to accept this small, stocky, genial figure with the direct, intelligent grey eyes and easy friendliness as the person he sought.

It was anyone's guess as to what Harper expected, but evidently the light-skinned man in the old floppy sandals and ragged trousers was not it.

Once they were engaged in conversation, Harper, Gomez and Father Cordoba, the New Englander's attitude changed. Father Cordoba's English was excellent, his perception, understanding, wit, keen and direct. But his willingness to do as Harper asked was a lot less than Harper would settle for. He offered a fee. Still Father Cordoba hung back. He wanted to be absolutely certain he would not be doing something for which he later on could be attacked by the police, the island's weighty bureaucracy, or anyone else. In short, as he stated it, what he needed wasn't the plea of Fitzgerald's heirs, it was an order from those in authority. Also, although as he said, the regular Father Superior was absent from

Feliciano – had been absent for six months now – it was still the Father Superior who must give the final permission.

Harper groaned, looked appealingly at his daughter, at Whitney, who were silent bystanders, and finally he turned to Roberto Gomez. 'You know the way around all this red-tape. *Do* something!'

Gomez used charm. It almost succeeded, for Father Cordoba was a man of charm himself and appreciated it in others. But evidently not enough, because he still insisted upon his former conditions. Gomez asked to use the telephone. There was none, he was informed. In the village, yes, but not at the monastery. Even Gomez rolled up his eyes. Then he tried an appeal to the priest's sense of fairness, but what finally worked was Dolores's mild statement.

'Father, my uncle endowed the school. Doesn't he deserve special consideration for that? He was murdered; won't you help us lay his soul to rest?'

Alfonso Cordoba smiled, patted Dolores's

shoulder and nodded. 'Of course. Is the body at Constable Beadle's office?'

They all thought it was, but when they walked back through the village, again to be stared at by a silent and growing crowd of peasants, they discovered, when they located Beadle, that the body, due to the heat and humidity, had been moved to a stone cellar when it had been learned the van from San Juan would not be along.

Beadle took them to this place; it was one of the few genuine cellars in Feliciano, and had been constructed, so Father Cordoba and Constable Beadle averred, to store ammunition during the early, bloody days of the island.

It was dank and dark and brooding. Dolores had to steel herself for the descent, and once they were down there, guided by a sickly torch in the hand of hulking Constable Beadle, she clung to Whitney.

Father Cordoba conversed briefly and in rapid Spanish with the constable. He in turn gazed upon Detective Gomez with a sour, enquiring expression. Gomez nodded without speaking.

In the far corner where the weak light touched upon it once or twice, was the covered form of a body. Whitney took Dolores back up out of there into the sunlight, and hot though it was, the daylight was very welcome. She said. 'It's – barbaric – what they have to do.'

He was sympathetic. 'But it should be done – soon.' He did not elaborate. He did not have to.

A refreshing breeze came down the dusty, broad avenue and a nut-brown middle-aged man who wore trousers hacked off a little below the knees, and discoloured old sandals, walked past and dropped a grin and a wink at Whitney, who smiled back.

At Dolores's look of inquiry Whitney said, 'A fisherman; an old friend. In fact, one of the first friends I made after landing on the island.'

'One of your informants about the Angelina Montoya affair?'

'Well, yes. But actually his father, who is quite old, is a better source of information.'

'Whitney, do you suppose we ought to explain about that to Mister Gomez?'

'I don't see why. It has nothing to do with your uncle's passing, and would probably only muddy the waters.'

'You're right of course,' she murmured, and turned as her father emerged from the cellar, followed by Beadle, Gomez and the little Father. They all looked solemn, but they all looked in accord, which meant that Father Cordoba would do what must be done.

Chapter Eighteen

A QUIET INTERLUDE

Dolores's father rode back to Estate Sao Paolo in the Land Rover with his daughter and Whitney Jackson. Gomez had remained behind in Feliciano with the little priest and Constable Beadle. He had not said why he'd done this and no one asked.

It was still quite early in the day, and after depositing Dolores's father out front of the *hacienda,* Whitney took the vehicle round back and parked it. There, he told Dolores he ought to get back to his cottage. He had been absent three days.

She demurred. 'Why? There is no one there waiting for you.'

'Well,' he answered, speaking slowly, 'I suppose just to be alone for a bit. To do some thinking.' He smiled. 'If no one else would understand, you should. Too many things have happened. It's like all the past and present ganged up and dropped upon my shoulders within forty-eight hours. For your father, even for Hernan' Godoy and Gomez, there has been just a murder. Do you see?'

She saw, and she also understood. As if all the travail wasn't enough, there was also the love they felt for each other to further complicate things. She said, 'All right. But when will you return?'

'When do you want me to return?'

She smiled. 'As soon as you get there and can get back.'

He bent, she lifted her face, they kissed. When he pulled back and started to turn she caught him. 'What are you doing?'

'Walking.'

'Don't be ridiculous. Take the car.'

His eyes were sardonic, but gentle. 'I never cared for bossy women.'

She dropped her hand from his arm. 'By

all means walk. I was only making a suggestion. Anyway, if you drive you can get there and back, sooner. And I *do* love you, so I'm entitled to want you back soon. Or is that being too bold as well as too bossy?'

He laughed, reached up to touch her cheek, then said, 'You're spoiling me with all this riding. Okay, you keep watch when the moon rises. I'll come to you then.'

Her father came through and out on to the rear patio as the Land Rover sped away. He looked, first, at the still, lithe figure of his daughter out in the sunlight, then he turned and deliberately watched the Land Rover bounce along on the rutted little road leading towards the promontory.

He lit a cigar.

Dolores caught the motion and turned. She saw her father blow smoke as he gazed after Whitney Jackson, and being far from insensitive, she could almost read his thoughts just from his stance, and his stare. She turned and slowly walked towards him.

In the shade of the patio, with a faint

breeze coming from the south, the direction of the old fort and the green-blue sea beyond, it was balmy and pleasant. Distantly, men whistled as they worked amid the citrus trees. The sounds were not of song; Puerto Ricans used the whistle in much the same manner as Mexicans or other Latin Americans. It could signify approval, admiration, pleasure, but it was just as likely to signify derision, sarcasm or refutation.

Dolores smiled at her father and he smiled back, his eyes, like her's only narrower and less intent, probing for whatever lay behind her look.

'You are fond of him,' he said, making it a statement instead of a question.

'I'm in *love* with him.'

The cigar gave forth a little burst of smoke. Harper removed it, checked for ash, then pointed towards a pair of chairs. As they sat he said, 'It's all very distressing, Dee, and I'm sure he's been an enormous help.'

She was patient with him. 'I was in love with him before, Dad. That's what we were talking about out there on the cliff the night Uncle Howard was killed. It isn't just something that happened as some kind of reaction.'

'I see. Well, of course you *are* of age.' He checked for ash again, ostensibly at any rate, before he said, 'What do you know about him?'

'He was a C.I.A. agent.' Her father gave a little start. 'And while he was escaping from Cuba a gunboat strafed them and killed his wife.'

Harper removed the cigar and held it low while he gazed steadily at his daughter. 'A widower...?'

'Yes. He has a stone cottage down near the shore.' She thought of the other secret they shared, debated whether to mention it too, then thought it would only do for her father what it had already done for her – muddy the water, as Whitney had said.

Her father leaned back very gingerly. 'Is he

still a spy?'

'No. For something like four or five years he's lived alone down on the beach.'

'And what did your uncle think of him?'

'He didn't really know him until the night of the party. But he liked him. He said so; but more than that, he *showed* that he liked Whitney.' Dolores looked over at the rugged, granite-jawed New England profile. 'Will you give him a chance, Dad?'

He coloured slightly, as though caught holding some questionable thoughts. 'Of course, Dee. Anyone you like – *I* like.'

She smiled. 'But I don't *like* him. I *love* him.'

Her father plugged the cigar back between his strong teeth. 'Well now, I'm not prepared to go *that* far with any young man you fall in love with. We New Englanders prefer the word respect to the word love.' He winked. 'But if you insist, I'll *try* to love him. Sentimental hogwash though, if you ask me.'

'You love me?'

'That's different.'

'And mother.'

'No comparison at all.'

She turned as a servant came out silently and stood waiting to be noticed. 'Yes?'

'There is a telephone call, *Señorita*. It is Father Cordoba.'

She and her father exchanged a look, then both rose at the same time.

The voice that came down the wire to Dolores was as bland, as pleasant and calm as always. Father Cordoba had only called, he said, to wonder if he might not come to the plantation that evening. She assured him no one would be more welcome. She also hesitated upon the verge of asking what he had found, if anything, during his post mortem examination of her uncle. But she couldn't make herself ask, and Father Cordoba acted disinclined to say anything over the telephone. In the end she rang off and went to the living-room where her father was impatiently pacing, and told him everything the priest had said.

His reaction was predictable. With customary Yankee aggressiveness he said, 'Why wait all afternoon? We can drive down there and hear everything within an hour.'

She demurred. 'Whitney isn't here. I want him to hear it too.'

'We can go and get him, Dee.'

'No. We'll wait.'

'But it's ridiculous to waste time like this.'

She gave him that very sweet smile, and he, unlike Roberto Gomez, knew what it presaged. After all, he was her father, had known her all her life. He made a great flapping motion with his arms, turned and dropped upon a couch.

'All right, child, but I must say after only three weeks in this place you're already acting like one of those lackadaisical natives. *Mañana*. As they say in Mexico – always *mañana*. Tomorrow.'

She turned, saying, 'I'll get you some of the local beer. You'll love it.'

She left the room, turned once in the doorway and saw him look moodily at his watch, then lift his eyes to the soft blue sky visible out of a window. She smiled to herself and continued on to get his beer.

He was entirely different from the natives, and yet in San Juan, which was a very cosmopolitan city, there were hundreds like him. If he'd remained there he probably wouldn't have felt much different, but Estate Sao Paolo was a kind of blending of two ways of life, and actually a man like her father did not belong to either, so inevitably he felt a little lost, a little out of place.

When she returned with the beer she could announce that the servants were preparing luncheon. That seemed to cheer him nearly as much as did the beer, although he approached it with considerable wariness and candid suspicion. It actually was nearer to being ale than beer. Puerto Ricans, at least in their locally-produced intoxicants, seemed to strive for quicker euphoria than imported U.S. beer offered. But their home-produced liquor was really quite good. It was only when one encountered sediment near the bottom of the glass one turned a little less than enthusiastic.

He was relaxed. 'It has now been four days,' he told her, holding the beer-glass away from his lips, 'and no one has been arrested. It's a good sign.'

She couldn't agree. 'What's good about that? I want that murderer revealed, Dad.'

'I was thinking, Dee, it was a good thing, after four days, that you and Mister Jackson haven't been arrested and hauled off to San Juan to be held on suspicion.' He sipped, peered into the bottom of the glass, uttered a slight grunt and put the glass from him.

She smiled. Any other time she might have laughed at his sudden expression of dismay. The sediment in the bottom of Latin American beer or ale, or stronger liquors in fact, had never been known to kill people, but every *norte americano's* reaction to it tended to indicate otherwise.

He then said, 'This Inspector Gomez is very skilled.'

'What did you expect?'

'Well I've been in Mexico, you know, and Panama, and some of the other places down here. You don't very often find men like this Gomez. I like him.'

This time she did laugh. That was Gomez's stock-in-trade; it was his charisma. He was forward, candid, pleasant, confiding. 'I thought I heard you two arguing in here this morning,' she said, 'when I was out back with Hernan' Godoy the overseer.'

'Well, lawyers always haggle with policemen. Neither would respect the other if this were not so. Anyway, I was simply getting in my bluff before he got in his.' Her father smiled. The so-called beer was working. 'Nice chap. So is Whitney of course. If I hadn't said that you'd probably put larger chunks of sediment in my next beer.'

The telephone rang. It was Fred Gore calling to offer in his languid, superior way, to come out and console her. She said, 'I wouldn't think of taking you away from the pleasures of San Juan. Anyway, my father is here, and along with Whitney, I'm managing quite well.'

She returned to the living-room to explain who Frederick Gore was, and to also state that she couldn't stand the sight of him. Her father listened, studied her a moment then said, 'Maybe you *are* in love. I can't recall ever hearing you say you detested a young man before.'

A servant came to say luncheon was ready. It was well past noon, but that too was part of the custom of Puerto Rico. At least out back, although in sophisticated San Juan and one or two of the other bustling, large cities, the U.S. Mainland traditions held true.

By two o'clock Dolores was beginning to wonder when Whitney would return. By four o'clock, with the sun slightly off-centre in its azure field, she was impatient for dusk to arrive so she'd be able to detect the lamps of the returning Land Rover.

Her father went to take a nap. He said, with some chagrin, that only a couple of days in Puerto Rico and he was already going native.

The house was still, peaceful, empty. It was the first time since the murder that she had felt the full weight of her uncle's absence. And yet, when she crossed to the front patio where a breeze blew, she could almost hear him driving up out front, climbing from one of the older, battered Land Rovers and clumping on up to the house.

It did not occur to her at that time, but later it did: her uncle now belonged to island legend. Doubtless, in time, it would be whispered that when the hot season arrived, he would return to inspect his groves and pastures.

There was nothing fearful about this, in native eyes. Rather, it was a nice, comfortable blending of life and death which in native views were pretty much one and the same.

Chapter Nineteen

THE MYSTERY DEEPENS

Whitney returned very soon after the sun had set. He confessed to Dolores on the rear patio where she'd gone to meet him, that he might have come back sooner except that he knew she'd be watching for the headlamps, so he waited an extra half hour, or until it was dark enough.

She told him about the priest's telephone call, and his nearing visit, then they went on inside where supper was waiting.

Her father made a valiant effort not to appear too curious, but not being a deceitful person his best efforts at subtlety failed. What he obviously sought was some personal information from the young man his daughter was in love with.

It was quite probable that Whitney understood this because he answered without seeming evasive, even volunteering information now and then, although as Dolores saw on the sidelines during this brief exchange, it looked as though he did not enjoy answering personal questions. But then whoever did?

She finally gave her father a stern look and headed their dinnertable conversation into other channels. Each time afterwards her father would begin to skilfully lead the topics back where he wanted them, using a courtroom-lawyer's practised methods, Dolores was right there, his worthy opponent, gently usurping the initiative and keeping everything on an impersonal, casual and serene basis.

When supper was over and her father had to go to his room for a cigar, she took Whitney out on to the rear patio where a great moon made everything almost as bright, but in a different way, as daytime sunshine could, and there she apologized for her father, explaining why he'd acted like that.

Whitney understood. 'In his boots I'm afraid I'd have been much tougher. There's nothing to apologize for. I like him. He's got your best interests in mind, and I'd like anyone who did that.' He slid an arm round her waist and led her over to the very edge of the patio, beyond the overhang-roof where they could see that spectacular Puerto Rican moon. It was still early but once the sun fell and darkness came, it did not *seem* early.

He said, 'You know – I have a little problem. As heiress to the Estate Sao Paolo you are a wealthy woman. As I've already explained, about all 1 possess is the stone cottage and ten or twenty acres of squatted-on land which, I think, actually lies within the boundaries of your plantation.'

'Does it matter?' she asked, leaning close to him.

'Of course it matters, love. Anything that affects our relationship matters very much.'

She had to agree, but right at that moment she couldn't have cared less about the estate, her uncle's wealth, or even Puerto Rico. She was being hypnotized by that enormous, eerie pewter moon.

'Just tell me you love me,' she whispered, but before he could tell her that or anything else they both heard the car coming. She turned, feeling irritation; why couldn't Father Cordoba have waited a little longer!

But it was Chester Morrison, her dead uncle's secretary who had been on the Mainland since before the murder, and when he saw her, met her father and acknowledged the smile and nod of Whitney Jackson, Morrison said he'd come as quickly as he decently could, but that there were some details he had to first look after in New York.

Then he sat down, loosened his tie, and the others explained what had happened while he leaned back and listened. His only comment afterwards was: 'Incredible. Simply incredible. I just can't believe it happened. He was so active, so healthy. He actually had been growing younger the past year or two. What a terrible waste for a man like that to die in such a fashion. It's simply incredible.'

Dolores had a question, and Morrison was the only one who probably could answer it for her at Estate Sao Paolo. 'Was Uncle Howard in love with Rosaria Aldama?'

Morrison looked at her a moment. 'You know, Miss Harper, despite the very close and warm relationship your uncle and I had, I was still his employee. Personal issues were not discussed between us.'

Dolores was not rebuked. 'But surely you saw them together. Surely you had some idea of their relationship.'

'I would say your uncle was fond of her, yes. And I am quite sure she was fond of him. She seemed to scintillate, if you know what I mean, when he was around.'

Dolores knew *exactly* what he meant.

Her father took over this aspect of the conversation with one question. 'Who in your opinion, disliked my brother sufficiently to want him dead?'

Morrison shook his head as he switched attention. 'Mister Harper, that kept nagging me all the way back here. I just cannot imagine anyone feeling that way towards him. Nor any reason, unless of course it was something like robbery, some crime by a burglar caught in the act. Something of that nature.'

Harper shook his head. 'No one seems to believe it was anything like that, Mister Morrison, for a very good reason; there were no strangers at the party, and no burglar in his right mind would attempt robbing the study with half the elite of this part of the island just outside the door.'

'Then I simply can't imagine who would do such a thing,' reiterated Morrison.

Whitney Jackson said: 'McFall? He was the first one through the door after the shot.'

Morrison shook his head at Whitney. 'Not Frank McFall; he and Mister Fitzgerald

266

were friends. Not close friends, you understand, but acquaintances. They were not in any sense competitive. I can't imagine any reason for McFall to be resentful. None whatsoever.'

Dolores couldn't either. In fact, over the past few days she'd ticked off each person who'd attended the party for a possible suspect, and had come up with just exactly nothing. Now Chester Morrison was adding to her nothing.

Harper said, 'I don't like this, Mister Morrison. I'm not a vindictive man, and yet I don't want to see this killer get away.'

Morrison was bland. 'He won't, sir. Puerto Rican police are surprisingly good. And after all, as I understand it, the killing only took place a little over four days ago.'

The front door chime sounded. Dolores gave a little start. For the moment she'd forgotten Father Cordoba. Whitney rose saying he'd go, and Dolores caught the way Morrison picked up this easy familiarity. She would of course have to explain to her dead uncle's secretary that the murder of his employer wasn't the only change that had taken place at Estate Sao Paolo since his business-trip to the Mainland.

Father Cordoba entered wearing a small deferential smile. He began apologizing at once as though he thought he had interrupted some critical council. Dolores and the others, excepting Chester Morrison, assured him otherwise. She offered to get him a drink. He declined, so did the others with the exception of Morrison, who excused himself on the grounds of travel-weariness, and after a bit the little priest was properly fitted in to their group with all the amenities taken care of.

He could see the others were watching him, waiting for him to speak. He delved round in a pocket and brought forth a bit of dull lead which he held up for inspection upon his palm. Dolores's father leaned and squinted.

'What is it?'

'The object that killed your brother,'

stated the priest.

'Ahhh; the bullet?'

Father Cordoba lowered his hand, examined the object he was holding with an intentness Dolores thought showed puzzlement, and said, 'No, Mister Harper, it is not a bullet. At least not in the modern context. It is a pistol ball.'

Harper looked blankly at the priest. 'Bullet, ball, a matter of semantics, Father.'

Cordoba smiled apologetically. 'No; I would have to disagree. A bullet, to me at any rate, means something made of steel and propelled by an explosive charge contained in a cartridge-case. Mister Gomez gave me that definition. You see, personally, I know very little about weapons of any kind.' He held up the piece of round lead again. 'This thing was not propelled by a cartridge full of gunpowder. Powder, yes – black gunpowder.'

Whitney Jackson gave a start. 'McFall said to me that when he first entered the study he smelled gunpowder. It sounded a bit odd at the time, but I didn't question it.'

Morrison, Harper and Dolores were gazing without comprehension from Whitney to the priest and back. Whitney spoke on, directing his attention towards the priest as though seeking confirmation.

'It was a pistol *ball*. It was fired from an oldtime weapon. The kind one charged by hand, then dropped the lead pellet in on top of the charge before firing the thing. Nothing else leaves that strong odour of black gunpowder in a room.'

Father Cordoba nodded. 'You are correct.' He offered Whitney the smashed bit of lead. 'Mister Gomez determined that this is exactly what happened. We did not arrive at such a conclusion simply when I removed this piece of pig-lead from Mister Fitzgerald's body. There were also powderburns on the flesh. A great many of them. Mister Gomez said that type of pistol, while terribly inaccurate was also very dirty to fire. To make certain a target was hit, a person had to hold such a weapon almost at arm's length towards the target, then yank the trigger. In this manner the particles of burnt powder were also driven into the skin.'

Whitney handed the antiquated pistol-ball to Morrison, who fished round for a pair of black-rimmed spectacles before closely examining the object.

For a few moments no one had anything to say. All Father Cordoba's revelation had done was add to the mystery, not enlighten anyone.

Whitney stared at Dolores as though looking through her. After a moment of this he said, 'Father, did Mister Gomez have any idea why someone would use such a weapon?'

Cordoba shook his head. 'None, except to speculate that such a weapon would be very difficult to trace, as opposed to a modern weapon that police ballistics would locate with relative certainty.'

Dolores's father lit a cigar, stared a moment at the lead ball Morrison was examining, then said, 'I think it has to go deeper than that. If a pistol like this was used, and assuming that the person who used it knew enough about such things to properly load it, then he would have some special reason beyond fear of ballistics detection, for employing it. Perhaps there was a personal involvement of some kind, either with the killer and the weapon or between my brother and the killer – and the weapon.'

Father Cordoba looked politely at Harper without speaking. Dolores, trying to find something that would help in what the men tossed back and forth, felt quite baffled.

Morrison offered the pistol ball to Harper for examination, but the dead man's half-brother shook his head refusing to touch the thing.

He said, 'Father; where is Mr Gomez now?'

'When I left, he was using the telephone in the village to call San Juan and speak to some weapons' expert down there.'

'Then perhaps he has a theory?'

'Mister Harper, all he told me was that it was crazy. That as far as he knew none of the guests at the party were gun-collectors, and certainly, as far as his experience with killers was concerned, he had never before heard of one who would take such a chance of botching the job. He seems to know quite a little about those oldtime muzzleloaders, sir, and when he told me such a weapon stood as good a chance of misfiring as it did of actually going off, I felt inclined to agree... This is a very crazy thing. If I hadn't found that ball no one could have convinced me the killer had used such an uncertain weapon.'

Morrison removed his glasses, pocketed them and said, 'Mister Fitzgerald had two of those old pistols in his desk. One was found here in the house when he was remodelling. The other one was a present from someone... Former governor John Gore, I believe.' He gazed at Dolores. 'With your permission I'd like to look and see if they are still in the desk.'

She nodded and Morrison left the room. They all watched him disappear into the study without saying a word. Each of them seemed to finally realize that Fitzgerald's slaying was now more than ever a genuine mystery.

Moments later Morrison returned silently, placed two rusty, ungainly little ugly weapons upon a table and threw up his hands. 'There they are. Smell them, gentlemen; neither has any scent of having recently been fired.'

Chapter Twenty

DOLORES AND WHITNEY
GO VISITING

Detective Gomez arrived at the plantation the very next morning and Dolores showed him the pair of little old pistols Chester Morrison had brought from the study.

He examined each weapon in turn, shook his head and put them aside. He said it was problematical whether either of them had been fired in a hundred years.

When Whitney came striding in with Dolores's father, Gomez greeted them with a small smile. 'I have a riddle,' he confided, in that pleasant, unorthodox manner of his. 'It isn't the gun that killed Mister Fitzgerald that troubles me – I suppose there are probably a thousand or more of those antiques hanging on pegs in dens and parlours all over the island as souvenirs of our blood-curdling past; my riddle is – why such a weapon?'

Whitney nodded and Dolores's father, in the act of lighting a cigar, said nothing until he had a head of smoke rising. 'It occurs to me,' he said, speaking slowly and gazing straight at Gomez, 'that perhaps it was an accident. Suppose someone who perhaps felt my brother was interested in those old things – perhaps knew he already had two of them – brought a third one to the party to either give to him, or show to him, and in the course of looking at the gun, it went off and struck him in the head.'

Gomez began nodding before Harper had finished. 'Then where is the weapon now?' he asked, having obviously already thought of the same thing.

'If the other person were in the room, saw the accident and for some reason panicked, thinking he might be implicated, grabbed up the gun and fled...?'

'No,' smiled Roberto Gomez. 'I'm afraid it won't hold water, Mister Harper. I had some similar thoughts yesterday so I made a very exhaustive investigation into the background of the one man who possibly could have brought some such thing off: Frank McFall.'

Harper pulled smoke. 'No motive, Inspector?'

'None whatsoever, Mister Harper.'

These two shared a rapport unlikely to be found among people who were not vocationally experienced in murder cases.

Harper said, 'Psychosis, Inspector; any trace where McFall is concerned?'

'None, I'm sorry to say. The only person at the party who has any kind of police record, even for misdemeanours, was Frederick Gore, and his record was for the things one usually expects from gay blades who drive too fast, drink too much, have too much money.'

Harper said dryly, 'But there had to be a hand on the trigger of the pistol that killed my brother, Inspector.'

Gomez would not deny that. 'Whose finger, Mister Harper?'

It was pointless to continue this kind of fencing. It also seemed quite pointless to speculate, yet that was all any of them could do, so they went right ahead doing it.

Detective Gomez left a little later; he had been reached by Rosaria Aldama's private physician, who had said he might now come to the Aldama plantation and interrogate his patient, but only very briefly, as any mention of the death of Howard Fitzgerald was sure to agitate her all over again. The physician did not, however, feel that a recurrence of the nervous breakdown was likely because by this time, almost a week after the murder, she had come to accept Fitzgerald's death.

Dolores's father got a telephone call from his office in Massachusetts; something to do with a rather extensive pending litigation, he explained after taking the call. He would have to go to his room and spend an hour or two writing instructions to his associates.

Dolores had the golden locket in her pocket and showed it to Whitney saying she felt it really should belong to Angelina Montoya's descendant, Rosaria Aldama. He agreed, at least to the extent of saying that whatever Dolores wished to do with the locket was perfectly agreeable with him.

'Could we drive over?' she asked. 'By the time we arrive Mister Gomez should be finished and gone.'

'Well...'

'Her physician told him she was much better. And I really think that telling her we know where her grandmother is buried would be a comfort to her. After all, she *has* had a fixation about the location of the grave all these years.'

Whitney gave in, but when they were standing beside the Land Rover he said, 'You know, if Angelina, who never married, is Rosaria's grandmother ... I'm not too clear on those things, but wouldn't she actually be Rosaria's grand-aunt, or great-aunt, or something like that?'

It seemed irrelevant to Dolores. A hundred and ten years was a very long time. She climbed into the car and smiled at him. 'You're very nice,' she said. 'I anticipated more of an argument about driving over there.'

He couldn't restrain the grin. She reminded him, at that precise moment, of a little girl. As he was climbing into the car Hernan' Godoy drove up to ask some questions concerning the cattle, which were to be worked this day. Dolores looked blank. She knew nothing about cattle except that they gave milk and were edible. Whitney surprised her by mentioning spraying the animals. Godoy looked surprised too. After he had driven off she said, 'Spray – cattle?'

He punched the starter, made a gesture of exaggerated ability, and grinned. 'I learned that much in Cuba. If you spray them every month or two parasitic flies and other insects do not bother them so much.' He engaged gears and started down around the house towards the front drive.

She said, looking as though she might be teasing – which she was, 'You are so knowledgeable and wise I just don't know what I'd ever do without you.'

He looked around quickly, detected the sly look in her eyes and made a quick grab which she fended off, then they both laughed.

It was a beautiful morning. Except when it rained – rather often as a matter of fact in Puerto Rico – every morning was golden, fragrant, faintly stirred by trade-winds, and wonderful to be out in. As they drove along, in no haste, she felt quite at peace. Like Rosaria, except that her shock hadn't been nearly as great, Dolores was beginning to put the pieces of her life back into some kind of order after the death of her uncle. It was inevitable for everyone who had known him, sooner or later, and in her case Whitney Jackson made it possible for the transition to be made sooner.

This time they did not have to skirt

around the village, and as they were moving carefully through the streets, where people and animals moved with a leisurely attitude indicating wheeled vehicles were not very common, Dolores thought she saw old Gregorio pass into a hovel not very far from the adobe cathedral. She uttered a little sound of surprise. Gregorio was supposed to be back at the stables caring for the horses.

If she hadn't been distracted this past week she would have known whether that could have been Gregorio or not, because up until the passing of her uncle not a day had passed that she hadn't visited the stables.

Whitney said it probably hadn't been Gregorio; that since most of the old men in this part of the island looked and dressed pretty much the same, and since she'd only caught a glimpse, she'd probably made a mistake in identity.

She didn't argue the point. It wasn't important anyway. But she felt privately convinced that it *had* been Gregorio. She also promised to make sure when they got back to the estate.

Whitney took a left turn and began the slow climb to the Aldama estate's front gate. This time, as she approached, Dolores was impressed. She had time to be and there really was less to keep her mind otherwise occupied.

She said, just after they passed the gate and could see that pillared mansion on ahead, dead-white in its dark, emerald-green jungle setting, 'It's absolutely beautiful. I don't think I've ever seen a picture of a plantation-residence as handsome.'

He nodded without adding anything to her superlatives. No one, driving through the main gate and heading towards that distant mansion, could fail to be enormously impressed.

There were no other cars in sight, out front, which seemed to support her earlier contention that when they arrived Detective

Gomez would no longer be on hand.

The place had that same pervading silence she had noticed on her first, and former, visit. It would, under normal circumstances, have been a sensation of ageless and unchanging serenity. There was some of that feeling now, except that there was also the sensation that grief was intermingled.

They left the car, went up the wide, shallow steps, crossed the broad gallery and Whitney raised the knocker. The same impassive *Carib* houseman admitted them who had turned them away that other time. He did not smile although he said if they would be seated in the reception room, to which he showed them, he would go at once and inform his mistress they were calling on her.

Dolores made a slight grimace. 'He reminds me of an automaton.'

Whitney was studying the age-darkened oil portrait hanging above the fireplace upon the opposite wall, of a dark-eyed, narrow-faced man whose gaze was calm and grave, and perhaps a little sad as well. He looked very distinguished with grey above the temples and a casual hand, long and sensitive and patrician, lying atop two thick books.

'A Montoya,' Whitney said softly.

Dolores also turned her attention to the portrait. 'He seems sad... Could it be – an Aldama – perhaps the one that...?'

A tall, thin, elderly man entered the room silently. He crossed over and offered a hand as both Dolores and Whitney rose.

'I am Doctor Martin,' the elderly stranger said quietly. 'Please excuse my intrusion, but it was by my orders that news of callers should come to me first. You will under-stand I am sure.'

The physician was a pleasant, quiet man, with a degree of iron in his make-up that showed only in the depths of his dark eyes.

'We would only like to see Rosaria for a few moments,' said Dolores, and the physician bowed his head pleasantly.

'Of course. And I am sure you will not

upset her. It was a terrible shock to her. But I think she makes good progress as the days pass, and after all, all things *do* pass, do they not?' He turned and motioned. 'Through the hall, across the living-room and beyond, where there are two French doors leading to a patio. She has been told you are calling. I think she looks forward to seeing you.'

The doctor continued to smile gently. Whitney said, 'Was a detective named Gomez here this morning?'

'Yes,' replied the physician. 'An exemplary example of his calling, too. Very gentle and shrewd. I was out there with them. I must say he could extract information from a babe in arms.' The physician's smile deepened in obvious respect for Roberto Gomez. 'She took it all very well. I had doubts, at first, but now I am sure she is on the road back.'

He walked ahead of them as far as the hall, then stepped back as they crossed over into the huge, cool and luxuriously-furnished formal living-room. Beyond, where two

French doors stood ajar, it was possible to see Rosaria. If they had expected to find some kind of invalid sitting disconsolately in a chair, wan and wasted, they were surprised, for she was standing with her back to them gazing out over the eternally shady park lying behind the great house.

But she was dressed from head to heel in black, and there was a small rosary dangling from one hand. To Dolores she seemed almost transparent over there where no sunlight reached; almost as though she were a figurine or possibly a full-length, motionless oil portrait. She knew, the moment that Rosaria would turn to greet them, her eyes would be holding that same strange soft-sad expression that were in the eyes of the ancestor, or whoever he was, hanging upon the reception-room wall above the unused little formal fireplace.

Whitney stepped silently over and held aside one of the French doors for Dolores. Rosaria turned, and Dolores was right. She gazed at them both, her beautiful golden eyes serene, resigned, shadowed by the depth of sadness that shadowed those other eyes in the painting.

She smiled and welcomed them, took them to chairs and sat facing them. She looked older and Dolores, who would have sworn there had been no grey in her ebony hair, saw some now, only a strand here and there it was true, but nonetheless, grey hair.

Chapter Twenty-One

THE STORY OF ROSARIA ALDAMA

It was one of those situations where no amount of small talk could intrude. Dolores sought for some subject to offer for discussion which would be agreeable to everyone, and found none.

Only one thing had brought these people together, held them together, and was uppermost in their minds. Rosaria asked when the funeral would be. Dolores replied that she would let Rosaria know as soon as she knew herself.

Then she brought out the golden locket and offered it to the older woman. Rosaria was interested, but until she found the tiny latch and opened the locket, her attitude was one of politeness more than curiosity.

She raised her beautiful eyes very slowly. Now, the gaze was not at all other-worldly, it was intent and sharp and searching. 'Can you tell me where you got this locket?' asked Rosaria.

Dolores turned to look at Whitney for that explanation, and Rosaria's eyes followed. The silence throughout the house was just as deep as ever, the attitude of gloom as pervading everywhere except upon the verandah where Rosaria said, 'I would like very much to know where this locket came from, because it belonged to one of my family.'

Whitney said quietly, 'It came from a grave. From around the neck of a woman – a girl – buried in a white lace dress who was wearing that locket, a brooch, and a golden bracelet when she died.'

Rosaria's face paled but that only made her eyes darker and larger as they stared at Whitney. 'You know where this grave is?'

'I know.'

'And you opened it?'

'Yes. I will explain if you'd like.'

'Please…'

He told of finding, first of all, the stone crypt, and later, during his brushing-out endeavours, stumbling upon that stone map in the crotch of a tree which led to the grave of Angelina Montoya. Not until he mentioned the name, did Rosaria nod her head.

'I have searched for that grave many years.' Rosaria's voice softened, turning both melancholy and tender. 'I offered a generous reward, but no one ever found it. I had no idea where it could be, although there was reason to believe it might have been down by the beach below the *castella barranca* where you found it. At one time, many years ago, I had men go down there looking. They found nothing. None of the searching crews found anything.'

'Why was Angelina so important to you?' asked Dolores. 'After all, she died over a hundred years ago.'

Rosaria leaned back slowly in her chair eyeing the younger woman. 'Everyone who knows of their ancestors has a favourite. But there are other reasons. For one thing, she was such a tragic figure. For another, she was my great-grandmother even though she was never married, and even though she died quite young.'

Rosaria smiled. She may, or may not, have noticed that this last announcement concerning Angelina did not surprise her visitors at all.

As though a fresh thought had just occurred, Rosaria swung her entire attention to Whitney. 'You opened the grave, saw the dress, got the locket – so you must also know how she died.'

Whitney nodded. 'A bullet, madam. She was shot in the head.'

Very slowly Dolores straightened in her chair. Her eyes got quite round and her expression seemed to congeal but she did not utter a sound as Rosaria, smiling a little in Whitney's direction, spoke again.

'I didn't doubt whose grave it was since I saw the locket, but you have just given me the final proof.' Rosaria dropped her head slightly and gazed at the golden ornament in her hand. 'I shouldn't have searched, shouldn't have tried so hard ... and yet all I wanted was to bring her into the family cemetery.'

Dolores said, 'Do you know who killed her, Rosaria?'

'Yes, I know. You saw the handsome man in the reception room above the fireplace? That was Francisco Aldama to whom Angelina was betrothed. My husband was descended from him through his second wife. Francisco killed Angelina Montoya.'

Whitney nodded gently, 'And the sailor, *Señora?*'

Rosaria looked surprised. 'You know quite a bit more than just the location of the grave,' she said. 'Yes – the sailor. He was Angelina's lover. I have of course heard the old legend of Francisco catching them meeting in secret, in one another's arms, and shooting Angelina, but I will tell you how this secret has been passed down in the

Montoya and Aldama families.

'Angelina and her lover had met many times. He was a fair, tall seaman who traded back and forth between Cuba and the mainland, often stopping in Puerto Rico.' Rosaria looked at Whitney with a little smile. 'That stone cottage where you live – Angelina's sailor built that.'

'That's where they met?'

'No. They met up there at the fort, but always late at night you must understand, for in those days there was almost always someone keeping watch for privateers. They met many times and over a considerable period of time, as he came and went in his ship. Angelina became pregnant. My grandmother was her child. Francisco Aldama, and no one ever blamed him, not even among the Montoyas, was driven to despair and madness so great was his love for Angelina. When he was told she was with child he took a little silver-engraved pistol with two barrels, and went forth to kill them both.

'Angelina was alone on the promontory

when Francisco found her. Exactly what was said, no one ever knew, but he told her to face him and she would not. She was standing up there looking out to sea. He shot her.'

'How terribly pathetic,' murmured Dolores.

'There is more,' Rosaria said. 'Francisco fled, and for a day and a half he ran howling mad through the jungle until *peons* found him and took him home where he screamed the story. But when the Montoyas and Aldamas went to the old fort, Angelina was gone. She was not there at all.'

Whitney said, 'The sailor…?'

'Yes. The reason Angelina would not turn and face her heartsick betrothed was because her lover was down below upon the sea rowing out to his ship. He heard the gunshot. He may even have seen Angelina fall. In any case, he rowed back ashore, found her after Francisco had fled, and buried her – but until now, no one ever knew where.'

Doctor Martin appeared briefly in the

doorway looking keenly at his patient, who smiled up at him as though to offer reassurance. He bowed very slightly, turned and departed.

This small interlude gave the guests of Rosaria Aldama a moment to organize their feelings and their thoughts. When the physician departed Dolores said, 'So much was known, Rosaria, you probably also know who the sailor was.'

The beautiful woman faintly shook her head. 'No. In those days, although the fishermen, humble, superstitious folk, often saw Angelina meet her lover, and even hid in the jungle watching as he built the little stone cottage, you must remember that fair-haired, tall *Yanquis* were greatly feared. No one would have voluntarily gone forth to this man. But they *would* keep their *patron*, Francisco Aldama, informed of all they saw. But no; to this day no one knows who the sailor was. All *I* know is that he was the father of my grandmother, who was born three months before Francisco Aldama killed poor Angelina Montoya.'

Whitney sat a moment in silence, gazing out into the ageless dark matting of jungle beyond the garden. 'Do you want to know who he was, *Señora?* It would take time and effort, but he could be identified.'

Rosaria smiled. 'No. What for? He has been dead a great many years, and I am sure that when he was put down into his grave a sordid, sad tragedy went down with him. He doubtless was the last one to die. First Angelina, then Francisco, who only lived six or seven years afterwards, and finally Angelina's sailor.'

Rosaria touched the locket with a very gentle motion. That exquisite, delicate portrait looked up at her. Rosaria smiled at it. 'She has always been my favourite progenitor. I was told as a child she was not a good woman, and of course she wasn't – in one way. Dolores? Can you imagine young and beautiful Angelina full of the fiery passions of the Montoyas, resisting the great love of her existence? Neither can I. And so, she is a sad little ghost whom, so legend says, used to attend every party given at the Estate Sao Paolo where the Montoyas lived at the time of her passing.' Rosaria smiled again, softly, gently. 'I never knew why she would do that because certainly she didn't expect to find her sailor among the guests.'

'Perhaps,' murmured Dolores, 'to forgive Francisco?'

Rosaria leaned suddenly, touched Dolores's hand, then leaned back. 'You are perceptive. I knew it the moment I saw you. That's what I've always thought; Angelina came looking for poor Francisco. And do you know, no one has seen her in a very long while now, not since I was a very small child in fact. I personally have never seen her, but my mother and grandmother saw her many times. So – perhaps she found Francisco, eh? Perhaps she got it all worked out and could then go away.'

Whitney cleared his throat and it had the effect of making Rosaria look at him with her expression changing again, this time assuming the gentle, ironic, understanding look of a woman who knows how such things as she'd just said must sound to a man.

She waited a moment, then said. 'Howard Fitzgerald was intrigued by the legend of Angelina and her sailor. When he was remodelling the old house over at Estate Sao Paolo he found an old pistol in a strongbox built into one of the walls. No one even knew the strongbox was there. Not that it held anything important, just that old pistol.

'Howard came at once and showed me the weapon. He thought it might have been the one Francisco used to kill Angelina. Of course it was not. In fact, I knew nothing of the pistol at all. Probably even whoever put it in the old strongbox forgot about it.'

Whitney said, 'You sound very certain it was not the pistol.'

Rosaria nodded. 'Very certain. *That* pistol was in the Aldama family for a very long while. Everyone knew which weapon it was. There was only one like it. It had silver engraving on it and an ivory handle.'

'Where is it now, *Señora?*'

Rosaria smiled at Whitney. 'I think you know where it is, Mister Jackson. I think you know that when Mister Gomez called this morning I gave it to him.'

Whitney nodded and slowly rose from his chair. He said, 'Dolores, we shouldn't stay too long.'

Rosaria sat looking up at them both. 'Please come back to see me,' she pleaded. 'I – particularly want the company of you two. Will you come back?'

Dolores bent, brushed Rosaria's cheek with her lips, squeezed one of Rosaria's hands and promised to come back. She then permitted Whitney to lead her from the room, across the other rooms and out of the house. She had blurry vision and a great lump in her throat.

She made no attempt to speak even when they were in the car heading for Estate Sao Paolo and Whitney did not force a conversation.

The sun was up there, pale yellow and hot,

making itself felt. There was no little breeze either, so the heat was punishing except for the last short distance up the drive to the *hacienda* where a dusty little car sat out front; there was shade along here.

As Whitney halted the Land Rover, not taking it round back as was customary, but stopping it behind the other car, he leaned, lay a hand upon Dolores's clasped fingers and said, 'Mister Gomez is inside with your father, I think. Are you up to it?'

She was. The drive back had been adequate to let her emotional disturbance subside. 'I'm up to it.'

They crossed the patio hand-in-hand, entered and felt instant, blessed coolness. Dolores's father and Detective Roberto Gomez rose and gazed at the younger people when they came quietly into the large, shady living-room.

'You have seen Rosaria Aldama?' asked the detective.

Dolores nodded as she took a chair and Whitney, standing near her, said, 'We saw her. We just came from there in fact, after an enlightening conversation.'

Gomez and Dolores's father exchanged a knowing look before the detective said, 'And do you know what happened?'

Dolores shrugged a little but Whitney nodded his head. 'I think so, Mister Gomez. But there is something I can't fathom.'

'Yes?'

'What happens next?'

Gomez resumed his chair and began nodding his head. 'Precisely, Mister Jackson – what happens next. Well; I don't know. I have never in my life ever even *heard* of such a thing, let alone been involved in anything like it. Maybe *you* can tell *me* what happens next?'

Whitney held forth one hand. 'Do you have the little pistol?'

Without a word Gomez brought from his pocket a silver-engraved little double-barrelled pistol with an ivory handle and handed it over.

Chapter Twenty-Two

DEATH IN PASSING

Whitney said, holding the little weapon, 'She brought it to Howard Fitzgerald. Her gift to him because, as she told us, he was intrigued by the tragedy of Angelina and the unknown sailor – who could very possibly have also been from New England. Most of them were, in those days, I've heard.'

Whitney held the small weapon upon the palm of his hand so that Dolores could see it plainly. In its day it had been the very latest model of an exquisitely engraved and ornamented weapon costing, no doubt, a sizeable amount of money.

Whitney said, 'It is too bad Francisco didn't lose it when he fled screaming into the jungle after shooting Angelina. But of course he obviously didn't, and so when he was found the gun was taken from him, perhaps pushed far back in a drawer or some other place where it wouldn't be seen.'

Gomez nodded. 'All supposition, Mister Jackson, but I think this is about as it happened. No one will ever be able to prove otherwise, but even so, the salient facts are unchanged.'

'Rosaria Aldama told me this morning she was very much in love with Howard Fitzgerald.'

'So she gave him the little gun?'

Gomez nodded. 'He excused himself from the dance hall to take it into his study, perhaps to put it in a drawer.' Gomez paused. 'The door was closed. We don't know exactly what occurred because no one saw it happen.'

Whitney broke in. 'Mister Gomez; there are two barrels, one above the other. When Francisco shot Angelina a hundred years ago he used the ball from one barrel.'

Gomez nodded again. 'Exactly. And afterwards, the little gun was put away. Everyone forgot. Rosaria Aldama gave it to the man she loved. He was standing there in front of his desk in the study. He cocked it, perhaps to ascertain that the mechanism still functioned – I have done that same thing many times with antique guns – only this time the barrel was pointing towards his head...'

Dolores let her breath out very slowly. *'That's* how it happened,' she whispered. 'Then – no one killed Uncle Howard.'

'He did it himself, accidentally,' said her father. 'That's what Inspector Gomez and I were sitting here discussing when you arrived.'

Slowly, Dolores's brows lowered in puzzlement. 'But no one afterwards found the gun.'

Gomez contradicted that statement. 'Yes they did. Not McFall, who rushed in, saw the dead man lying there and called out what had happened. Father Cordoba might have discovered it, but he would not move the corpse. Then you and Whitney drove up outside, you see, and everyone rushed out back to tell you. All but one.'

Dolores remembered which face had been missing that night. She said, 'Rosaria...?'

Gomez took back the little weapon from Whitney and moodily regarded it. 'Yes. All but Rosaria Aldama. She went in there. She told me this morning that she knelt to kiss your dead uncle, and there was the little gun, beneath him. She took it.'

'To conceal what happened?'

Gomez looked at them all. 'No, I don't think so. It was not her fault. It was no one's fault that in a hundred years nobody ever thought to remove the second charge from this damned gun.

'She took the weapon for an altogether different reason. It was an epitome of evil to her. She was stunned, horrified, out of her mind with a slowly descending grief. She took the gun because for the second time it had brought grief to the same house – and to her, as the last member of the Montoya family.'

Dolores's father worked at lighting one of his expensive cigars. He was pensive. In his world nothing like this was possible. Murder yes; it happened right along. But not such a murder as *this* one had proved to be.

Gomez said. 'And so – we come back to the question you asked when you first came in, Mister Jackson – what happens next?'

They waited for Gomez to resume speaking. It was a lengthy wait. He was neither a callous nor cruel man. He could even have been a bit of a sentimentalist, which was not unheard of in detectives, even in seasoned, career-detectives.

'Well, I shall return to San Juan and file my report. Mister Howard Fitzgerald was accidentally killed while examining a small oldtime pistol.'

Gomez looked up and waited, expecting someone to say something. No one did, not right away at any rate, but after a bit Dolores's father spoke through a small cloud of bluish smoke.

'The law deals in facts and only facts. The

little gun Rosaria Aldama gave to my brother was a keepsake in her family. Beyond that there are no facts.' He gazed at his daughter and at Whitney Jackson. 'Do you follow what I am saying? Angelina Montoya disappeared over a hundred years ago. No one was ever brought to the bar for whatever happened to her, so the facts are simple and explicit: the gun that killed my brother was an antique weapon which was very unfortunately still loaded. Those are the *facts* as we *know them to be*. And that's all there is to it.'

'Even though,' said Dolores, 'Whitney and I can show you Angelina Montoya's grave; show you that she was shot in the head?'

Gomez and Harper had evidently already covered this because after they looked at one another Gomez said, 'Can you prove to us, Miss Harper, that this gun in my hand is the weapon that killed Angelina Montoya – a hundred years ago? No? Well then you see, what you really have is a woman in an old grave, and a little pistol, but no verifiable connection because leaving out old gossip, no one can prove *now* that any of this happened *then.*'

'Even if it could be proved,' put in Whitney, 'what would be the point?'

Dolores's father nodded vigorously. 'Precisely. Mister Aldama, allegedly the murderer, is beyond punishment. How would justice, or any other social amenity, be served by going to all the rather considerable expense of proving, or *attempting* to prove, Mister Aldama murdered the woman he very desperately loved?'

Dolores suddenly rose and ran out of the room. The men sat a moment looking after her, and while ordinarily at least one of them would have been baffled, now they said nothing and for a moment avoided looking at one another.

It was perhaps appropriate that her father should break the silence. 'She has always been a person who felt things very deeply. Please excuse her.'

Roberto Gomez spread his hands. 'There

is nothing to forgive.' He was motionless a moment then dropped his hands and said, 'Well, that may not be right either. Maybe they *all* need it. Francisco Aldama needs forgiveness, Angelina Montoya needs it…'

'Rosaria Aldama?' suggested Whitney.

'Yes, and Rosaria Aldama,' assented Gomez.

'And what happens to her for taking the gun away?'

Gomez pocketed the little weapon almost with a gesture of distaste. He looked at Dolores's father. 'It is called concealing evidence, interfering with the police in the performance of their duty.'

Harper looked away, refrained from agreeing, and smoked.

Gomez lifted and dropped heavy shoulders. 'It goes into my report.'

'I'd like to make a suggestion,' said Whitney. 'Did you meet Rosaria's physician over there this morning?' When Gomez nodded Whitney said, 'Ask him to also write a report to be filed alongside your report,

Mister Gomez. Rosaria wasn't herself; in fact for several days she probably did not know anything at all. What she did was done under a variety of emotional disturbance only a medical man – or a woman capable of loving someone very much – would be able to explain.'

Gomez smiled, rose and offered Whitney his hand. 'I had that very thought in mind.' They shook and looked directly at one another. Gomez said, *'Patron; estado* Sao Paolo should have you for its new master.' He turned to Dolores's father extending the same hand. 'Mister Harper – *vaya con Dios* – walk with God.' He then stepped back towards the front doorway and said, 'Please – if you will tell Miss Harper…?'

After Gomez was gone the two men in the living-room were mostly silent. Harper eventually said, 'I can't fathom why such a thing was allowed to happen, Whitney. I believe my brother must have loved Rosaria, and she certainly loved him… What could it be? Is it possible that a thing as inanimate as an old pistol could somehow catch some of the frenzied madness of its last owner, and when someone else touched it over a hundred years later…?'

'No,' murmured Whitney. 'The anguish was more than enough for everyone to completely overlook the fact that the little gun had *two* loads, not just the one that killed Angelina.' He turned as Dolores appeared in the hallway entrance. 'Are you all right now?'

She nodded, smiling slightly. 'I am ashamed of myself. Has Mister Gomez gone?'

'Yes,' said her father, and looking from one of them to the other, he said, 'and now, if you'll excuse me, I must finish that correspondence to my office.'

After Harper had left them, Whitney took Dolores in his arms, held her close for a moment, then took her gently out to the back patio.

She said, 'What about the *other* grave?'

He answered quickly. 'Leave it. Opening

one Pandora's box is enough – *quite* enough – to last me a lifetime.'

'But you wanted to know about the holy man, Whitney.'

'Not any more I don't. If I've learned one thing from all this it is simply that the past belongs to the past, and if the present intrudes, some very shocking and unnerving things occur.'

She turned as someone paced out of sunlight into shadow over by the stables. It was old Gregorio, and he was holding the dusky hand of a short, quite stout woman whose ebony hair was shot through with great amounts of grey.

'He *was* down in the village,' said Dolores.

Whitney smiled. 'The *peons* have a saying: happiness does not belong exclusively to the young.' He bent and swept her cheek with his lips. 'Are you going to scold him for not staying home?'

She moved closer shaking her head. 'Do you suppose he will marry her?'

'Why not? It's a very old custom in Puerto

Rico. The requirements are simple: people only have to be in love.'

'Well, in that case, Whitney, would you marry *me*?'

'Certainly *Señorita*,' he answered in Spanish spoken slowly and carefully enough for her to understand. 'Since it is the first such proposition offered me today, I will of course marry you. And in the years ahead I shall prove myself that most formidable of all husbands to you.'

'All you have to do,' she whispered in English, 'is love me.'

'Will it be easy, *querida*?'

She looked up instantly. 'Why wouldn't it?'

'The Estate Sao Paolo, your own wealth...'

'If you'd like I'll give them away.'

He laughed. 'Don't be hasty. I think we can somehow make the adjustment to wealth and serenity – and love.' He squeezed her and they turned to stroll out where a giant catalpa was losing its cabbage-sized pale flowers, one petal at a time.

She said, 'Whitney; what of the *third* grave down below the promontory – the most recent one?'

'I can't forget, Dolores. I doubt that I will ever forget. But as I said before, that belongs to another chapter of my life. It is far behind me. It will never interfere between us.'

She accepted that exactly as she accepted everything else he said, because she knew him well enough, finally, to understand that he was a very honest, decent kind of a person.

'And Rosaria...?' she asked softly.

He was slower answering for the basic reason that there was no simple answer. Rosaria Aldama, beautiful, wealthy, thoroughly dazzling though she undeniably was, had lost a great part of something that had shone from within her, with the death of the man she had loved.

Age, held off so long, would not be held off any longer, and love, which she seemed capable of giving only to the kind of man

Howard Fitzgerald had been, might find another such man, but all the odds were overpoweringly against it.

He had to say, 'I don't know, Dolores. I wish I could find some reason for what happened, but I can't. All we can do, it seems to me, is go visit her often and help her back.'

She liked the way he said that. It showed his depth of compassion and understanding.

Old Gregorio slipped forth from a cool, shaded part of the stables with his fat lady-love, and, without noticing that he was being observed, set his floppy old hat on his head at a devilish angle, hooked his lady's great arm through his, and started jauntily along the path which led in the direction of the village.

Dolores watched a moment then raised her eyes. Whitney was whimsically regarding her. He said, 'Well, *patrona*, do you order him back at once to his work?'

'Once, when I was riding past one of the

labour crews, and before one of them trilled that little warning whistle they make when an outsider approaches, I heard someone sing out in Spanish that Gregorio was an old rooster.'

Whitney laughed aloud. 'If you can't be a *young* rooster, why then I suppose the next best thing is an *old* rooster.'

'And you?'

He scooped her up in both arms sweeping her off her feet. 'Try me, Lady Of The Forest.'

She reached to pull his face down and fiercely kissed him. 'All right, I *will* try you!'

The sun was reddening again, beginning its long glide towards the blue-green place in the far off sea where it sank each day, and throughout both jungle and groves of Estate Sao Paolo flashing-coloured parrots complained.

The publishers hope that this book has given you enjoyable reading. Large Print Books are especially designed to be as easy to see and hold as possible. If you wish a complete list of our books please ask at your local library or write directly to:

Dales Large Print Books
Magna House, Long Preston,
Skipton, North Yorkshire.
BD23 4ND

This Large Print Book for the partially sighted, who cannot read normal print, is published under the auspices of
THE ULVERSCROFT FOUNDATION

THE ULVERSCROFT FOUNDATION

... we hope that you have enjoyed this Large Print Book. Please think for a moment about those people who have worse eyesight problems than you ... and are unable to even read or enjoy Large Print, without great difficulty.

You can help them by sending a donation, large or small to:

**The Ulverscroft Foundation,
1, The Green, Bradgate Road, Anstey, Leicestershire, LE7 7FU, England.**
or request a copy of our brochure for more details.

The Foundation will use all your help to assist those people who are handicapped by various sight problems and need special attention.

Thank you very much for your help.